STD

DO NOT REMOVE
CARDS FROM POCKET

THE GOLDEN THORN

THE GOLDEN THORN

HELEN F. DARINGER

Illustrated by Kurt Werth

New York

HARCOURT, BRACE AND COMPANY

LIBRARY OF CONGRESS CATALOG CARD NUMBER: 56-5873

PRINTED IN THE UNITED STATES OF AMERICA

CONTENTS

THE GOLDEN THORN

I

MARK

THE BABY puckered his mouth to cry. He was a plump baby, almost too big for the swaddling clothes in which he lay wrapped, and his wail was lusty.

From the flat doorstone where she sat braiding rushes for a mat, Mary stretched a slim, sun-browned hand to set the low hammock swinging, half in bright autumn sunshine, half in the thin shade of the gnarled old fig tree that hugged the wall.

"Bleating like a hungry lamb as though your mother had not fed you!" Mary made pretense to scold, but her voice was coaxing. "Noise enough to fetch the old tax gatherer from his counting house! Hush now, before he shuts you up in his dark wallet."

Then as the crying continued, shrill and insistent, she let fall the rushes and took up the child and whispered soft things. The crumpled little red face relaxed, the sobs dwindled to puffy, purring sighs.

"You are spoiled, sir, that's the trouble." Mary waggled an accusing finger at the diminutive nose. "Do you think I've nothing to do but coddle you all the day?"

Satisfied with the world now that he had got his own

way, the child yawned and blinked, his drowsy gaze upon the face which bent close and comfortable above him. It was the face of a young girl, scarcely seventeen, tall for her age and slender, with chestnut-colored hair and eyes of so intense a blue under the shadow of their lashes that when she was a child her father used to tease her.

She could be no daughter of the land of Judea, Simon would declare, solemn as a Pharisee on the Sabbath. For the children of Judea were born with eyes dark as the fall of night. Early on the morrow morn, yes, before the sun had climbed above the mountain, Simon must go seek a proper black-eyed little girl for himself, though he might have to journey as far as Bethlehem or Gibeah to fetch her.

Not for an instant was his small daughter deceived by the threat. Underneath his beard she could see a smile crinkling, she knew he would never part with her. But she would cover her face with her hands and run to her mother, for it was a kind of game the three of them sometimes played by early starlight before the hour for sleep.

Did Damaris think it might be, Simon would turn to question Mary's mother, that some Phoenician trader, hawking his spices and woven stuffs from door to village door, had stolen their child from out the crib and left in its stead this blue-eyed changeling from his saddle-pack? Phoenician merchants had ever been sharpers at exchange.

Or perhaps a Roman soldier, or a Greek mercenary making his way inland from the coast over the mountains to Damascus or Jerusalem, had laid a spell of mischief upon

4

the child, to turn her eyes blue as the wild iris that stars the valleys in springtime. For it was said that in the city of Caesarea, where the caravans brought their bags of grain and bales of silks and incense to be loaded upon Roman ships, there thronged sorcerers from Egypt and wizards from Chaldea who trafficked in spells and magic.

What though the sorcerers asked a dear price for their secret spells? If a Roman legionary had a whim to dabble in magic, dabble he would, however much it might cost him in silver. . . . Could Damaris recall whether any soldiers of the legion had chanced through the village while the child was yet a babe in the cradle?

To the little girl leaning against her mother's knee in the cool of the evening, the very syllables which Simon spoke were sorcery. At the sound of his words dark figures began to take shape, conjured out of the dusk. Egyptians with rods like serpents came crowding closer and closer along the narrow dusty street, and shadowy Chaldeans rose tall as the fig tree, whose long beards curled silken black over the folds of their jackets.

Mary shut her eyes to see more clearly, and then was more than half fearful to open them lest the shapes might after all be real. She liked to scare herself, it was exciting, and sometimes she did it even when there was nobody near to protect her.

"Shall we claim this changeling, Damaris?" Simon was asking. "Or shall we have us a new daughter?"

"You have to keep me!" Mary pounded with both fists

upon her father's knee. "It's me that keeps off the evil eye. Don't you 'member, Father?"

Damaris brushed her cool fingertips against the child's cheek. "Softly, little girl, softly. You know your father is only teasing."

Simon continued to stroke his beard as though deliberating what his reply should be. "It is so," at last he would concede with a judicial nod of the head. "The color blue has virtue against ill luck. Yes, Damaris, perhaps we might do worse than keep the changeling."

And then he would swing Mary suddenly off her feet, high into the air, and she would laugh aloud, excited and gay, and neither of them paid any attention to Damaris' soft voice saying that talk of magicians and the evil eye did a child no good. Could not Simon think of a gentler game to play?

But that had all been long ago, while Damaris was still with them. After her death Simon's mother had come to tend the house and look after the child until she was well grown. She was a kind woman, the grandmother, giving Mary much freedom, but grave and still, not inclined to laughter. Now she had returned to the village of Bethlehem to dwell with her daughter, and the household had a new mistress. Late in the spring, when the season of rains was at end, Simon had brought home a new wife.

Two or three years earlier, a summons had come from one of Herod's priests for Simon to present himself in Jerusalem. A skilled stonemason, his labor was required for a period upon the great new Temple which King Herod was building. It was there in Jerusalem that Simon had found himself a bride, one of his overseer's several daughters, Miriam, only a few years older than Mary.

At first Mary had been pleased to have a companion of so nearly her own age in the house. In the fifteen or twenty flat-roofed dwellings which sheltered along the shoulder of the hill, flanking the narrow street with their walls of sun-baked brick or stone, rough hewn or white-plastered, almost everyone was middle-aged or elderly. The younger ones had been obliged to seek employment in more prosperous communities, the girls in households of the well-to-do in neighboring villages, the boys sometimes journeying as far as Jerusalem or Damascus, where work was plentiful and wages were paid in coins of silver and bronze. Had it not been for eighteen-year-old Mark, whose father's illness kept the youth at home to shepherd the flock and harvest the stony patch of barley and wheat, Mary might often have been lonesome.

Many a long afternoon her grandmother had permitted her to spend in the steep craggy pasture above the village where Mark was herding his father's score of sheep and black-speckled goats. Nor were the afternoons idly spent. From his shepherd's wallet the tall, quiet boy would draw a rolled scroll or a page of papyrus which the rabbi had lent him, for the old rabbi was a man of learning. Together Mark and Mary would con the writing, trying to get by heart the vast knowledge it set forth, of how to reckon with

7

numbers, of stars in the heavens and rivers in their courses
and of that strangest of all the beasts of creation, the mighty
Leviathan which dwells in the depths of the ocean.

Often the two would practice the Latin language, which
Mark was learning from his father. In a world ruled by
Romans, his father maintained, any man who hoped to ad-
vance his fortunes must be able to speak the Roman tongue.
Abel himself had acquired it in youth, working under a
Roman master in Damascus. Abel was ambitious for his
eldest son.

Mark too was ambitious, though not for the things which
his father wished for him. His desire was not for gold to
buy land and flocks. He longed to become a man of learning, a scribe who could converse with scholars and win the
respect of the wisest of the elders. But a sick man must be
humored and kept quiet of mind, and Mark could not
openly set his will against his father's.

Only to Mary could he talk of his plans and dreams. The
rabbi, although he prized knowledge, would have held that
it was Mark's duty to obey the will of his father. Let Mark
see to it, the rabbi would have exhorted him, that the flocks
were multiplied and the pastures extended. Leave it to one
of the younger sons to become a scholar if any of them
should be so inclined.

It meant no small thing to Mark that Mary encouraged
his ambition and argued for his right to make his own de-
cision. Not that any argument could ever have prevailed
upon Mark to turn his back upon what he believed to be his

duty. But obedience to his father in this, Mary tried to make him understand, was not a question of duty.

"Why should it be your responsibility more than your brothers', just because you happen to be the eldest?" she demanded to know, stooping to shove away a fat, unwieldy lamb which persisted in nibbling at the leather thong of her sandal.

"What's to keep your brothers from seeing to it that the pastures are increased and the flocks doubled?" The struggle with the balky lamb had left her breathless. Her face was flushed, a lock of hair flopped in a moist half curl against her forehead. "Let them inherit your father's land, Mark; they are minded to be prosperous plowmen and shepherds. But it is you that your father will one day be proudest of, you'll see," she promised, so earnest he could but believe her.

While they talked, Mary quick and eager, admitting of no obstacles, Mark thoughtful, more restrained of speech, the sheep scattered and strayed unnoticed and the nimble goats mounted from rocky ledge to ledge far up the steep hillside. The Latin phrases the two had been rehearsing about buying and selling and "What are your orders for today, sir?" were forgotten, and the rabbi's scroll neglected with the wise sayings of the ancients.

"You must take employment with a rich man, Mark," Mary would urge. "One with a library so you can read all the books. Don't you think an Arab merchant would be best?" Her eyes as they met his were a deeper color than the folds of the blue-woven shawl she wore thrown over her head as shade against the sun.

"Remember what the rabbi is always saying—that there is more scholarship among the Arabs than the Romans." (The rabbi had no use for Arabs, he was not praising them; he was dispraising the Roman overlords of Judea.) "A rich Arab would be in luck to employ you in his shop, Mark."

"I'd count myself lucky to tend his horse and sleep in his stable." Of wider experience than Mary, Mark could assess more clearly the opportunities likely to be open to him. "Rich men don't give stable boys the run of their libraries." He laughed a little, ruefully, but his eyes were bright.

"All I ask is to earn enough to buy a few sheets of papyrus. Then I shall set myself up in business on a street corner as a scribe. With the hundreds of workmen there must be for the Temple, there ought to be letters and tallies a-plenty to write. Though from what I hear"—again the little deprecatory grin, as if to make light of his own optimism—"there are already more scribes camping in the streets of Herod's city than there are laborers for the building."

In spite of the enthusiasm with which Mary encouraged Mark, she could not hide from herself a sorry wish which she would have been ashamed to own. If only Abel would not too soon recover his health! For once Mark found himself free to seek the city of his dreams, who could say when he might return?

II

MIRIAM

FOR A TIME Mary had attempted to persuade herself that it would not greatly matter when the day of Mark's departure came, now that her father had brought home a bride. Miriam would be company enough.

Miriam was young, she would laugh with Mary at the glassy-eyed impudence of the hairy black goat, straining at its tether to spy upon them as they stirred the lentil stew for supper. Miriam would keep their spindles whirling to tales of wonder as they spun the white wool from their distaffs into endless thread for the winter's weaving. The splendors of Jerusalem would lighten the grinding of the barley and wheat for bread—King Herod's great Temple, his towered castle upon the western hill, the columned palace where he held court within the city, and the vast amphitheater he had built in the valley below the city wall to make holiday entertainment for his Roman guests.

And Mary for her part would show Miriam the cove behind the hill where the lilies blossomed in springtime blue as a pool fallen from the skies, and anemones and wild geranium and the spreading rock-rose bloomed brighter of color than the rich silken stuffs the Syrian traders fetched in their saddlebags from the city of Tyre, scarlet and blue and yellow and lavender-pink.

The herbs that overhung the ledges she would teach Miriam, which kinds had power to cure aching bones, which a fever, and where to look for the sheep when they strayed, and higher among the outcropping rocks, the crags where the goats liked best to venture. The secret thicket of wild fig and thorn she would share with Miriam, where the young gazelle had fallen helpless with an arrow in its flank, and where every day until the creature was healed of its hurt she had carried a jug of water and armsful of green herbage plucked from the pasture. . . . Oh, they would be companionable as sisters together, Miriam and she, talking and laughing and telling each other their inmost thoughts.

Perhaps Mary expected too much of Miriam, or perhaps Miriam felt herself at disadvantage with the tall stepdaughter who welcomed her as an equal rather than with the deference which Miriam felt was her due as Simon's wife and the mistress of his estate. Or it may have been that she was disappointed to find herself presiding over so small and plain a household in so remote and poor a hamlet.

Whatever the reason and whoever was more at fault, neither took any lasting pleasure in the other. If Simon had been more often at home, things might have gone better. But his work had taken him to Gibeah to help cut stone for a bridge on the road the Romans were building, and it was only an occasional Sabbath he could spend with his family. With him away, Miriam was homesick for Jerusalem, complained of the dullness of the village, wished herself back among her sisters and cousins.

"Is it my fault the village isn't any bigger?" Mary would make reply under her breath. "Am I to blame because there are no shops?" The impatient shrug of her shoulders, the noisy clang of the bronze cooking spoon as she hung it upon the peg against the wall were eloquent of the exasperation which pride would not permit her to voice. "If you didn't want to live here, why did you marry Father?"

Mary resented Miriam's assumption of authority. Miriam, on the other hand, inexperienced, unsure of herself, accustomed to the rigid rule by which her own mother had governed, believed it was not merely her right to expect obedience from the daughter she had acquired with her marriage. It was her responsibility to improve Mary's character, to teach her that it is the duty of girls to be submissive.

"Unless you show a more docile disposition," the young stepmother prophesied, "no man will be willing to have you for wife. Meekness is a virtue required of women. I speak from experience, Mary." If there was in Miriam's tone more than an echo of complacency, not to say smugness, it might well have been forgiven in one who had herself so recently achieved the status of wife.

"Self-will does not become a woman, and even less does it befit a young girl." Miriam smoothed the thick coil of black hair that crowned her head and spread the fingers of first one hand, then the other, upon her knee to admire their whiteness before she took up her distaff again. "It is for your own good that I tell you, Mary. What's that you are saying?"

"Nothing," muttered Mary, half choked from the effort she was making to hold her tongue. "My foot struck against the bench, that's all." Self-will indeed! As though anyone in all Palestine had ever been more set than Miriam upon having her own way!

After the baby was born Miriam was too much occupied with mothering him to notice when Mary ignored some minor instruction—how small to cut the garlic root for barley stew, which of the two or three willow brooms to use for the stone-paved floor, which for the doorstep, or at what precise spots upon the shelf to place the leather bottles and wooden bread trough.

"How does she think we managed before she came?" Mary would question indignantly, chafed by the unaccustomed supervision and, it must be confessed, not unwilling to annoy Miriam by ignoring her commands.

Absorbed and happy in her infant son, Miriam felt more at home, was less inclined to assert her authority and saw less to find fault with in her surroundings. Though it did not occur to her to say so—after all, it was no more than Mary's duty to make herself useful—she was grateful for the capable if somewhat slapdash way in which Mary took over the housework. It would have required only a word of praise or an occasional "Thank you" for Mary to redouble her efforts to be helpful and quite forget past differences between them. But the word was not spoken.

Even so, there was a relaxing of tension between the two. Pleasure in the baby and concern for his comfort drew them together and made them forget their differences. Miriam would smile over the old leather stonemason's apron she was patching to observe how obligingly the infant let himself be lulled asleep by Mary's mimicry of a drowsy sparrow's chirping, or with how knowing a look he turned his head when Mary imitated for his entertainment the mournful *baa-a-a-ing* of a baby goat crying for its supper.

Now that Miriam had stopped issuing commands, Mary was quick to make excuse for her imperfections. "Her family probably pampered her more than was good for her. Maybe it was partly my fault we didn't get along. I must remember to let her have her own way," she resolved, not exactly conscience-stricken but eager to be friends. "It won't hurt me to give in to her—at least about things that aren't important."

The truce was not for long. As the infant grew older he seemed to smile more often to please Mary than his mother. Or so it appeared to Miriam, though she may only have imagined it. He was still so young, not yet out of his swaddling clothes, that it is doubtful whether he clearly distinguished one from the other.

Miriam's feelings were hurt. He was her child, he belonged to her. It was not fair of Mary to make him love her more than his mother. If only Miriam could take him away, go home with him to Jerusalem! Though even there she would not be allowed to have him to herself, she realized with a sharp pang of self-pity. People had always taken advantage of her. Her older sisters had made free with her possessions just because they were bigger and stronger than she, and her mother had let the younger ones play with Miriam's toys whenever they had a mind to. . . . And now Simon's daughter was taking advantage of her just like all the others, doing her best to win the baby away from her.

So now, on this afternoon in autumn when Miriam brought her distaff to sit on the doorstep in the sun to spin, the sight of Mary with the infant sharpened her sense of grievance.

"It is not good for him to be handled overmuch." Miriam looked older when she was in a bad humor, older and less pleasing of feature. "He needs his sleep."

Mary deposited the drowsing child in the low, loosely woven hammock and reached for a handful of rushes. "He was fretful," she explained. The threads must have got tangled in the new tunic Miriam was weaving, to make her act so snappish.

"Someone must be coming up the road," she remarked cheerfully, to take Miriam's mind off the tunic or whatever it was that had upset her. "The dogs have been barking these past five minutes."

"If someone came every time the dogs barked, this place would be overrun. Nothing ever happens, nobody ever comes. Why should anyone?" Miriam demanded with a scornful sideward glance at the crooked little street, hardly more than a rutted lane sunning its brief length between a double row of low, flat-roofed dwellings. "What is there here for anyone to see except a huddle of old houses on a rock, I ask you?

"There's nothing," she made fretful answer to her own question, "absolutely nothing!"

She could have wept, she was so tired of the poky little village, it was so empty without Simon, and she so longed for the stir and bustle of Jerusalem's crowded thoroughfares. Wherever you walked in Jerusalem now you would hear the sound of flutes and of children's laughter, and all the city would be festive and gay, for it was the time of the Feast of the Tabernacles. Every roof would have its bower of green boughs for the feast, and at dusk the lights would twinkle out over the city, golden as fireflies.

"Look, Miriam, there's someone coming—a soldier—two soldiers!" Mary was on her feet, one hand shielding her eyes against the glare of the sun. "Look, you can see the shine of their lances."

"Legionaries, and someone on a donkey." Miriam too had risen and was craning her white neck to see.

"It's a woman on the donkey, I do believe," Mary reported. "They're stopping in front of the tax gatherer's."

"Where else do you suppose? You weren't expecting them to pay us a visit, were you?"

The sarcasm was lost upon Mary. "Old deaf Esther has heard word of it and come out to see," she noted with a hasty nod for the wrinkled neighbor across the way.

In every doorway figures were appearing, women's heads

were thrusting out, and small boys were being forcibly restrained from swarming forth to throw themselves upon the
glamorous strangers. Like moths to a flame the burnished
long lances drew them, the short-swords dangling from the
soldiers' nail-studded belts beckoned them.

"It must be a surprise party." Mary giggled at her own
joke. The tax gatherer was notoriously unsociable; he had
no friends. "The publican is not dressed for company, his
hair is not combed."

The Romans delayed only to exchange a few words with
the publican before he pointed them on up the street. It was
the same angular pointing gesture with which on market
days he was accustomed to single out a shepherd or a crafts-
man to make demand of further tax payment.

The taller of the two legionaries took the lead, advancing
at a deliberate, easy pace up the stony pathway, his iron
lance tilted carelessly against his shoulder. Behind him
trailed the sluggish-gaited brown donkey, the long skirts
and out-thrust leather-shod feet of its rider visible behind the
legionary's broad back; and at the rear, a second soldier.

Miriam clutched Mary by the sleeve. "It's us they're after!"
Her voice trembled. "Why isn't Simon here to take care of
us!"

"Father has already paid his tax. It can't be our house
they are looking for. Or if they are," Mary asserted, by no
means so certain of it as she would have had Miriam believe, "we've no cause to be anxious. We haven't done anything."

She was not afraid, she told herself, stiffening her shoulders and planting her feet more solidly upon the doorstone, not really afraid. It was only that they were not used to seeing legionaries in the village, it lay so far from any main road and so high upon a hill. "Let them ask as many questions as they wish, they will not frighten me." And indeed a kind of uneasy excitement was beginning to make her cheeks burn and her pulses beat faster.

"Most likely they are only seeking a night's lodging for the woman." She hazarded an optimistic guess to hearten Miriam. "Probably she is mother to one of them."

Miriam had snatched up the infant to shield him behind Mary. Mary could feel against the back of her neck the sharp intake of Miriam's breath as they stood waiting in silence for the Romans to declare the purpose of their visit.

The taller of the two men brought his lance to rest upon the doorstone, careful not to disturb the half-braided mat of rushes at which Mary had been busied. His leather sandals were thick with white dust, for it was months since any rain had wet the land, and the stripe that bordered his tunic was dulled with the same sandy grit.

"Is this the house of one Simon?" It was a statement rather than a query. The Aramaic syllables had an odd sound coming from his Roman tongue, and he puffed a little from the steepness of the street. A powdering of dust grayed his round, cropped head and made him look older than he was.

"Let me do the talking." It was the woman who spoke.

"Here, Julius, here, Cato"—as peremptorily as though it were two children she was ordering about—"help me down off this beast.

"There's not a bone of me left whole," she complained in

her wheezy, old-woman's voice, gingerly testing her joints before she trusted herself to stand upright.

"The goat tracks these provincials are satisfied to call roads! It's a miracle the last tooth is not jarred loose from my head." She addressed herself to Mary who, for her part, could make but little clear sense of the flood of foreign words. The Latin phrases which she had been rehearsing with Mark had mostly had to do with affairs of buying and selling, needful for a youth seeking employment with a city merchant.

"And nothing but a rubble of old houses and tufts of thornbush on a bare ledge when you get here." The traveler gave the folds of her linen dust cloak a brisk shake to rid it of the clinging sand. "Take that, will you!" She slapped at a fly which buzzed too near her nose.

"Which of you, I ask, is of the house of Simon?" She glanced from one girl to the other as if it were some mischief she had caught them at, filching an almond cake from the pantry or a sweetmeat from the dish set aside for the master's table. Her eyes were small, round and shiny as a sparrow's, and deeply set in a net of fine wrinkles.

"We are both of the house of Simon," Mary informed her, lifting her brown head proudly and wishing that Miriam would bear herself with greater boldness. Why write your fear upon your face for Roman strangers to read?

"Miriam is the wife of Simon and the child is Saul, his son. I am Mary, the daughter of Simon's house." Suddenly she remembered her manners and the hospitality which is ever the due of strangers. "Will you enter, my lady? Let our house be your home for so long as it shall please you."

She fetched a basin of water and a towel for the guest to cleanse her hands and face of travel stains, and then a cup and clay pitcher, still cool from the deep, sycamore-shaded spring where it had been filled less than an hour since, that she might drink and refresh herself.

"The bread is well baked." The old woman praised it, breaking a second, larger piece from the flat, pancake-shaped loaf to eat with the goat's-milk cheese and dried figs which Mary set before her. "Nor the cheese isn't bad either, though it could do with a mite more thyme for savor."

"She approves of your cheese," Mary translated, attempting to put Miriam at ease. "Why don't you let her hold the baby while I carry a jug of water to the men? Old ladies always like babies."

But Miriam would not. Better risk failing in hospitality, her look warned Mary, than to expose an innocent infant to the attentions of a heathen foreigner.

Although the traveler obviously relished the food, she was enjoying even more the flattering interest with which Mary attended her every remark, upon whatever subject—the deplorable state of the roads in this part of the world, the cracked glass goblet which the Tyrian shopkeeper had tried to palm off upon her, mistaking her for a country woman (but she had been more than a match for him), and the scandalously dear cost of Egyptian grain in Pompeian markets.

"My master, I must tell you, will touch no bread except it be made of the finest Egyptian wheat." She pursed her lips and drew a long face, affecting not to countenance such extravagant taste, but it was plain to see that she was boasting. "My lord Sextus never questions the cost"—pausing to pick over the plate of dried figs to select the tenderest ones—"I must grant it to his credit. He's a true-born aristocrat, he spends freely."

It was not interest alone, nor yet courtesy, which made Mary hang upon the stranger's words. If she let her attention wander ever so slightly, to speculate whether there would be enough left of the loaf for supper or to glance through the door to see that the soldiers were still idling upon the doorstone, she lost both head and tail of the old woman's homely gossip. Concentrate as intently as she would, she could glean only a fraction of meaning from the garrulous Latin sentences. The rest she guessed at, or supplied from her imagination.

From time to time she translated for Miriam's benefit, to include her in the conversation, if conversation it could be called. The stranger's name was Lollia, Mary relayed the information to Miriam, and she was nurse to the younger son of an official named Sextus. The emperor had recently commissioned Sextus a quaestor, to visit various towns and cities in the provinces of Judea and Samaria to take an accounting of the public treasuries in order that Caesar Augustus might not be cheated of his lawful share.

From Jerusalem it was the intention of the quaestor to

journey to Callirrhoë on the eastern bank of the Sea of Salt. For it was said that at the hot sulphur springs of Callirrhoë cures might be obtained for illnesses of the bones and weaknesses which afflict the flesh. King Herod himself, so Sextus had heard, went often to the springs of bitter waters to seek relief for the secret malady which threatened to consume him.

"Your master then is in poor health?" Mary inquired as Lollia left off talking for a moment to take another nip of cheese.

" 'T is not the lord Sextus," the old woman sighed, "but my little master Rufus.

"The remedies we have tried"—she shook her head solemnly back and forth, fluttering the loose ends of ribbon that filleted her disheveled gray hair—"and all in vain! Herbs and lotions, prayers to the gods, hot salt baths and fare of fruits and coarse bread and fish such as the emperor uses to preserve his royal health." She sighed again, a gusty sigh. "Sacrifices in the temples, a snake-skin from the priest of Aesculapius to wrap about the child's thigh, to say nothing of the amulets and other rare charms fetched at great cost from shrines of Osiris in Egypt—and all to no effect.

"As the child grows, the lameness grows with him. Lively as a bear cub he is and strong, but the one leg drags wooden, having in itself no power of motion. So now we are bent to try what cure the waters of Callirrhoë will bring. The lord Sextus will not hear to it but that the leg can yet be made whole.

"Though this I confide to you in secret, for the master would not have it known," Lollia added, shielding her mouth with her hand that the words might travel no farther than Mary's ear. "No less a person than Apollonius, he who was one time physician to Caesar Augustus himself, declared when he made examination of the child it was a defect of birth, without remedy.

"Still, who can tell?" She spat a tough stem of fig into her palm and tossed it out the door. "Cures have been made before this without physicians, cures a-plenty. At Caesarea in the market place I was told of a root of rue so powerful if it be only brought to sick persons it quickly drives away those who are called demons. And who knows whether it may not be a demon that lames the child, or mayhap the evil eye of some envious slave?"

The figure of the younger soldier darkened the doorway. "Put halter to your tongue, old nurse," he charged her, making a playful feint with his short-sword. "Time runs away while you gossip, and there are yet the sealed money baskets to collect from the publican, both here and in the hamlet below."

"Is that any way to address your betters, Cato?" Lollia rebuked him, settling herself more solidly upon the bench. After a few minutes' delay, however, to prove that it was she and not the soldiers who would determine the time of departure, she brushed the crumbs from the lap of her yellow-dyed dress and got to her feet.

"You are acquainted with Sapphira, the herb woman in

the village below?" she asked Mary. "It was Sapphira who sent me here."

Ever since Mary could remember, the dark garments and white hair of the herb woman had been a familiar sight upon the heights of the hillside. Some of the villagers held that she was a witch, a white one, dealing only in good magic. Others declared that she had learned her cures of a priest of Mithras somewhere eastward beyond the mountains. This, however, was certain, as many a one could testify—there was in her a special kind of virtue, whether in the touch of her hand or in the balms and medicines she brewed, that could bring healing.

Meeting her sometimes upon a mountain ledge as she searched for herbs, Mary would exchange greetings with her and perhaps some talk of the weather and the flocks. But what, she wondered now with a quickening sense of expectancy as she assisted old Lollia with the ties of her dust cloak and helped adjust the peaked hood to her satisfaction, what had the herb woman to do with the Romans? And why had the herb woman sent Lollia here?

"She has promised me a root of the rue I was telling you of. We must stop by to get it, nor keep master Sextus waiting in Gibeah."

"Don't get excited," Mary cautioned herself, to quiet a breathless flutter within her chest. "Whatever it is, it has nothing to do with you."

"The young lord Rufus wears me out with his liveliness." Lollia took a step toward the door, the soldiers were growing restless. "At my age I am in need of a girl to help me. Sapphira gave you a good recommendation, Mary, yes, she praised you highly.

"You are mannerly, that I can tell. And dress you in Roman clothes, with a ribbon to fillet your hair, you would pass even in Pompeii for Roman born. Understand it is not every young girl I'd make the offer to. Nor you don't need to bargain over wages, either. Sextus is liberal of purse, the pay will be ample. Ah, my girl"—unexpectedly Lollia patted Mary upon the cheek, a quick little pecking pat, half congratulatory, half patronizing—"you may well thank your gods that this day I chanced upon Sapphira by the roadside.

"Pompeii is a wondrous fair city, I promise you, finer far than your stiff-necked Jerusalem, the streets paved smooth as your own floor for the lords to ride in their chariots, and my master's dwelling is fit for a king." Lollia was pleased with herself, pleased with Mary, and more than pleased to be making so marked an impression upon these two unsophisticated young provincials. "You'll see for yourself, my girl, whether Lollia exaggerates!"

"What is she telling you?" Miriam inquired suspiciously, coming a step closer. "What is it she wants of you?"

"But I could not—"

The old woman lifted a pudgy hand in imperious gesture to still Mary's protest. "Not today," she assured her. "I'll give you time to make preparations. We'll pick you up on the return from Callirrhoë. The lord Sextus will send an escort of two or three legionaries to fetch you in all safety, you can tell your father."

Mary fumbled for words. Even speaking her native Aramaic she would have been hard pressed to make coherent statement of the maze of thoughts confusing and exciting her, though of course, she kept telling herself, she could not under any circumstances accept the old woman's offer. Not if she wished to—nor was she at all sure that she did wish it—for her father would never permit it. He would never be willing to let her go so far from home.

"I could not—" The Latin words had failed her completely, and anyhow it was too late for them. Lollia had already been hoisted atop the donkey and was waving a farewell, her yellow sleeve flapping like a banner in a breeze.

"What did she say to you, Mary?" Miriam demanded to know, disapproving, suspicious, intensely curious. "Tell me. It is my right to know."

Mary's eyes were still following the Romans down the dusty street. "She proffered me work in Pompeii. She wants help with the little lame boy."

"Of course you told her you would not!"

"I did not tell her anything." It had been on the tip of Mary's tongue to say that nothing could induce her to go live across the sea among the pagan Romans, but she was ruffled by Miriam's officiousness. "I shall have to think about it," she said.

Of course she would not go. Leave her own village? . . . But Mark would soon be departing, now that his father was again in health. It would not be the same without Mark. There was still her own father— She could never bring herself to go so far from Simon. It would grieve him to the heart.

Miriam was disdainful. "Think about it indeed! Your father would never allow it. Nor will I."

"My father trusts my judgment; he will let me do as I think best. I shall have to think about it," Mary repeated, gathering up the rushes and half-braided mat. "I haven't made up my mind."

III

THE STAR

ALL DAY the household had been busy and even now, late though it was, a lamp still burned. Scattered across the pine table lay coverlets and garments which Miriam was folding into bundles ready for the saddlebags.

For Caesar Augustus had ordered a census taken to count the numbers of people under his rule from whom he could exact taxes in the various provinces. To make it easier for the census takers, the people of Judea had been commanded to present themselves before the officials of their native cities. Although Simon had long made his home elsewhere, he was by birth a native of Jerusalem and must return there for the tax count. Miriam and the child would accompany him.

It had been Simon's intention, and Miriam's too, that Mary should make the journey with them—the donkey could as easily carry two as one, and Simon would walk— but the black goat was ailing and someone must remain to tend it. Simon had the animal under one arm now, in the dark, earthen-floored little room which opened into the house, his other hand gripping the creature's long neck for

Mary to dribble down its throat a mixture of wormwood and warm olive oil.

"There, Nana old girl, stop bucking and kicking and stand still. You know I'm not hurting you." Simon swabbed his hands clean of oil with a bunch of grass from the manger. And to Mary, "Get Mark or Esther to help you if she needs another dose tomorrow. And keep her indoors. This winter air is bad for her."

"I'll fetch an armful of hay to bed her down warmer," Mary made excuse to step outdoors.

She had mastered, or thought she had mastered, the worst of her disappointment at being left behind. It was nobody's fault, it was not as though they hadn't wished her to go, she told herself. Someone had to look after the goat and you couldn't expect the neighbors to. A good goat cost dear, and it would be a heavy loss if Nana should die. Besides, though she had not a grain of sense and was obstinate as a donkey, you could not help being fond of her. Anyhow, you could not go off and leave a live thing to suffer. . . . Mary swallowed a lump in her throat, perhaps of sympathy for the animal, perhaps of pity for herself.

For a moment the tears welled so salty hot against her lids that she had to fumble with shut eyes for the mound of dried grass at the root of the leafless grapevine, and having found it, forgot the need for it and stood forlorn in her own darkness.

A sound roused her. Somebody was coming up the hill, by way of the street but by one of the steep goat trails.

It must be a shepherd, Jacob or Reuben or lame Levi, or maybe Mark, since it was they who most often stood the night watch over the flocks. Whoever it might be, it would not be a robber. Robbers haunted the highways or sought out villages where there were houses of wealth, and certainly there was here in this hamlet no family which was not poor.

It might be that the shepherds required aid for a disabled sheep, though they were more likely to be sending for additional cloaks and tunics to wrap them against the cold. The wind blowing down from the snowy heights would make nothing of a single cloak of wool, and the hours of a winter night stretched long with only rocks and thornbushes and juniper for shelter. Whatever his reason for coming, the shepherd was in haste. Mary could hear the iron sound of loosened stones rolling along the ledge as a foot struck against them, and the dry rattle of pebbles.

The village lay in darkness, a huddle of shadows, with here and there a milky glimmer where the starlight fingered a whitewashed wall. She waited, staring out into space, resting a hot cheek against the roughened bark of the old fig tree, seeing in thought her father take down from the iron hook above the goat's manger the saddlebags for Miriam to pack with the bundled garments.

Tomorrow night there would be feasting at the house of Joses, Miriam's father, in the upper room of which Miriam so often boasted. No wonder Miriam pined for Jerusalem.

Here in all the hamlet was not a single house with an upper room.

Many lamps would be lighted, the place would be bright, for a man as well-to-do as Joses would not mind what quantity of olive oil the lamps consumed. There would be talking and laughter, Simon would be given the seat of honor, and Miriam would be holding the baby for everyone to admire. Nobody would be thinking of Mary, sitting alone in an empty house with only old Esther and the sputtering light of a suet wick in a little clay dish for company.

"Hello there, hello the house!" A call summoned her from her reverie. "Is anyone awake in the house of Simon?"

It was Mark, pulling himself up over the stony ledge across the way where the street came to an end. "Is anyone awake, I say?" He was upright now, running with his shepherd's crook toward the house. "Simon, I say, hello there, Simon!" He pounded upon the door with his staff.

The door opened to let a shaft of light flicker across the doorstone.

"What is it?" Simon thrust out his head to see. "You, Mark?" He threw the door wide for the youth to enter.

"Is there danger? A threat of wolves and need of help?" Already Simon was reaching for his woolen cloak and the knotted stick in the corner. "Or has one of the flock broken a leg?"

"Neither." Mark was panting, he could hardly speak. "All's well with the flock."

"Are you ill, Mark?" Mary questioned anxiously behind

his shoulder. She had never known him to be so importunate, as if he were feverish.

"There is a star," he told them, the words breathless, "a star out of the East, a new star. Watching the sheep, we saw a new light in the skies. Jacob and Reuben have hastened to follow it—and I shall follow too. Levi stays to guard the flock. But I turned aside to fetch you, Mary, and you too, Simon."

Had a lamb been endangered upon a rocky height and Mark on the way to the rescue, he could not have been more urgent. "Quick, quick, else we fall too far behind."

Mary darted past him into the house to get her cloak. That he should have come so far out of his way on her account, and at the risk of losing the star, lightened all her dejection.

"Follow a star?" Miriam questioned him blankly. "What would that profit you?" She was incredulous. "Where would you follow it to?"

Simon dropped his cloak and knotted stick upon the bench. "Not tonight, Mark. We go tomorrow to Jerusalem for the tax census, and must be early on the way to arrive before fall of darkness. Some other night I'll go with you."

At ease again about the sheep, he rolled up his stiff leather stonemason's apron to stow in a saddlebag in case he should find employment in the city. "Now that you speak of it," he remarked, more out of politeness than from any real interest, "I recall that Daniel and Nahum made similar mention of a strange new light they noticed in the heavens some ten or dozen nights ago while they were standing their turn at night watch over the flocks. There's no view to be had of it from here, I suppose?"

"The shoulder of the mountain shuts it from sight. You must go beyond to see it." Mark had no time to delay for talk. "Are you ready, Mary?" In the guttering lamplight the shadow of his arm made a moving arc against the dimness of the low ceiling, like a great bird in flight.

"You are not thinking of going, Mary!" It was Miriam who spoke, shocked and peremptory. "A girl of your age keeping company at this hour of night with shepherds in the field!"

"It's nobody but Mark and Reuben and Jacob," Mary reminded her impatiently. "I've known them all my life, and Reuben is old enough to be my grandfather."

"It does not matter who they are." To one of Miriam's strictly orthodox upbringing, there was no distinction to be made between virtue and the outward conventions of behavior. "What would people think? What would they say! You speak to her, Simon. She will not listen to me."

He looked from Mary to his wife, and back to Mary again. "Miriam is in the right, daughter." He was reluctant to inflict a second disappointment. "It would not be seemly for a young girl."

Mary made no reply, but her eyes, meeting his, begged him to let her go. Something of the sense of urgency which had impelled Mark to trust his father's flock to the care of another while he set off in quest of an unknown star had communicated itself to her. Within herself she felt a great surge of longing to behold that strange star and follow through the night wherever it might lead.

"Be firm, Simon," Miriam pressed him, her voice mounting shrilly. "Tell her flatly she may not go." Even had Miriam not spoken, her presence would have been sufficient reminder that it was she, not Mary, who most swayed Simon's judgment.

Simon sought to soften his refusal. "Only be patient, daughter, and I myself will take you one night to see this new light in the heavens that Mark tells of. A week is not long to wait."

A kind of numbness thickened Mary's throat, making speech difficult. "I'll keep you company to the end of the street," she turned to tell Mark, the words almost inaudible. She refused to meet her father's eyes and her gaze passed over Miriam as though she were less than a shadow against the shadowed wall.

The flame leaped upward in the little clay lamp as Mary brushed past, her head high, her step swift, throttling as best she could her hurt and resentment.

"You must tell me about it afterward, Mark, all that happens. Miriam is a city dweller, she fears even the rustling of a leaf in the dark." Mary essayed a laugh, to make it appear that the friction between her and Miriam was of trifling importance, but the laugh caught in her throat.

The end of the street was soon reached. "It was kind of you to take so much trouble on our account," she made awkward attempt to thank him. "I would go with you if I could."

"I know," he replied, "I know." He was disappointed, but the disappointment was outweighed by an imperative desire to overtake Reuben and Jacob before it was too late.

She heard him go running along the ledge, heard the hollow echo of a falling stone that marked his passing, caught the faint sound of wind-borne syllables as he turned to cry a farewell before he went plunging on down the steep slope.

For some minutes she stood unmoving, listening to the silence that flowed back upon the mountain like a great slow wave after his going. There was no sound to be heard, no sound of watchdog barking nor cock crowing eerily in its sleep, no oxen lowing, restless in their stalls, no shepherd piping to his flock in the darkened field. And in the distance no fox nor jackal yapped, no wolf howled. Even the wind had ceased. In that still and empty air nothing stirred save her own sighing breath.

It was a lonely silence, intensely lonely. She shivered, though she was not cold, and pulled the rough woolen cloak tighter about her shoulders.

Overhead the stars hung like lanterns, so close it seemed she had but to stretch out a hand to touch them. The sky was growing lighter. She could almost see the brightness moving toward her where she stood, that same radiant brightness which was lifting the hills out of darkness to rise—height above snowy height—to the very heavens.

And somewhere far below her, unseen in the dim gulf of

the valley, a figure was hastening forward into that radiance
—Mark, loyal, warm-hearted Mark, stout ashen staff clasped
in his hand and shepherd's wallet belted at his side over
the threadbare goat's-wool cloak.

"Mary," her father's voice summoned from the doorway,
"why do you stand without?"

Now, while she watched, the light began to fill the valley
like a cup, brimming toward the darkened hamlet, drenched
in shadowed sleep, and the stony ridge where she stood.

"Come, Mary," Simon called a second time, more loudly. "Come, daughter. The hour is late and we must rest."

Slowly she turned, to take her way through the silence and darkness to the house.

IV

AS THE PROPHET FORETOLD

THE BUSTLE and stir of the departure for Jerusalem had faded into empty quietness. The ailing goat had been dosed and fed—Mary could hear the dry, soft-sliding swish and rustle of the hay as the creature foraged aimlessly in the manger—the house had been swept and made tidy again, the baby's crib pushed out of the way into a corner and the upright wooden frame of the loom dragged into position before the hearthstone, and still there was no sign of Mark.

She wondered as she stepped to and fro at the weaving whether the baby was missing her. By now they must have arrived at the crossing of the ways where the Roman road cut through on the way to the hill of Jerusalem. On a road paved level as that with stone, the baby would be joggled no more than in a cradle as he rode in his mother's arms.

If it had not been for Miriam—the thought repeated itself—if it had not been for Miriam and the way Simon always let her have the last say, Mary could have gone last night with Mark and the others to see the strange star. Nothing stays new forever, strangeness soon wears off, and the star would be an old story before Simon returned from

Jerusalem. Everybody in the village would have had a look at it except her.

The shuttle snagged in the woolen warp, and bending impatiently to free it, Mary noticed a gap in the pattern where the threads had been skipped. Now it would have to be undone, all the last hour's work, and the undoing would be twice as troublesome as the doing. Why should she be obliged to keep up the same old daily round of chores while Miriam went riding at ease along the highway to Jerusalem? Most likely they were not even remembering about how they had left her behind.

Mary yanked sharply at the cloth to pull the threads together. The cloth puckered, a warp thread snapped, the shuttle leaped from her hand to go bouncing across the floor. Whatever was it that possessed things to make them act so contrary?

Stooping, she retrieved the shuttle from beneath the stool where it had come to rest, smooth olive wood polished by long use to time-darkened ivory, and dropped it with a thump into a round clay dish on the shelf. "There," she addressed the offending shuttle, wadding in on top of it the tangle of brown-dyed thread, "unsnarl yourself if you can!" The weaving could wait until she had a mind for it.

What could be keeping Mark so late? Surely he would not have gone on home from the shepherds' field this morning without first stopping at her door. He would know that she was expecting him, waiting to hear what there was to tell. Could it be that he was still following the star?

She dismissed the idea as soon as it occurred to her. No star shines in broad daylight, and besides he would not long neglect his duty to his father's flock. Mark was not hasty of action like her, he would not forget about the sheep. You could depend upon Mark.

It was high time she made up the bread unless she meant to go hungry. What was left of the breakfast loaf Miriam had wrapped in a cloth with some cheese and an onion or two to sustain them on the day-long journey. To judge from where the sun stood above the fig tree it would soon be the hour for the baker to light the oven for the weekly baking, and if she was late with her loaves he might put her off until the last.

"You are young," he would grumble, "it will do you good to wait. The young must learn to practice patience." As though she had any desire to be patient!

She would have liked to refresh Mark with a serving of bread and cheese when he came, but he would have to do without the bread. There might be a few almonds left in the bin which he could have instead, or dried grapes in the jar, or figs.

The dough, a thick yellowish-gray mass, had stiffened in the clay bowl where it had stood over night. It stuck to her fingers as she turned it out upon the wooden bread trough to knead. And it was lumpy. Perhaps she had been in too great haste with the mixing, though a few lumps more or less would hardly matter, with only herself to notice. If the baker commented, let him. He must know as well as anybody that you can't always get the lumps out of barley dough. Nevertheless before Mary shaped the stubborn mass into balls the size of her fist she pinched and thwacked it passably smooth.

She was laying a stick of wood on the fire, burying it in the hot ashes—a green stick, slow to burn, since fuel was scarce and must be made to last as long as possible—when there came the sound she had been listening for, the thud of a wooden staff upon the doorstone.

"Are you here, Mary?" It was Mark, pushing the door ajar that she might see it was he.

"A minute later and I wouldn't have been here." She would not have him think she had had nothing else to do but wait all the morning for his return. "But enter, Mark, don't stand outside." The sun glancing through the half-open door brushed her chestnut-brown hair with flecks of gilt and threaded with bronze the faded dun-color of her dress. "Come in, rest yourself a bit.

"There's no hurry with the loaves, since there's none save me to need them. The others will be banqueting in the upper room at the house of Joses—fare fit and fine to tickle the taste of a king, no doubt." Hearing herself repeat the phrase which old Lollia had applied to her Roman master's table, Mary laughed a little.

Somehow, as she laughed, setting a cup of cold water upon the bare pine board for Mark's refreshment with an ostentatious flourish as though it were honey-sweet wine in a golden goblet, all her lonesomeness vanished away. "Figs,

Mark, to savor with the cheese, or dried grapes?" she quer-
ied, lifting the stone lid of the fruit jar. "Or shall I crack
you some almonds?"

"The cheese requires no savor," he thanked her, "and I
must keep an appetite for the lentil stew my mother will be
cooking." He laid his staff upon the floor beside the bench
and shifted the strap of his shepherd's leather wallet to let it
hang loosely from his shoulder.

Though she could tell from the way he sat that he was
weary, resting both arms upon the table, absently crumbling
a morsel of cheese between thumb and forefinger, it was a
weariness of the body only. His mind was intent upon some

45

experience of its own, at far remove from the low, white-washed room where she sat facing him across the narrow table. For a moment she had a curious impression that it was not she at whom he was looking, but someone or something beyond, visible only to him, of which he alone was aware.

"He's puzzling about where that star came from," she told herself, to explain away some indefinable change she was beginning to sense in him, of quality or of mood. "Mark doesn't take things for granted the way most people do. He wonders about why things happen and what the meaning is." Whatever the difference which might have come over him, she sought to convince herself, it could not be toward her that he had changed.

"In a minute or two he'll be himself again, the same as always." For there was about him a quality of remoteness, not so much a withdrawal upon his part as a going beyond her, which made her increasingly self-conscious and ill at ease, as with a stranger.

"Tell me about last night." She reached for his cup to refill it and took a handful of dried grapes from the jar to lay before him on the table. "I hope coming up here didn't make you fall too far behind."

Mark lifted the squat, clay-colored cup to revolve it carefully upon his palm, like a potter appraising the shape of his handiwork. Almost unconsciously Mary observed, as more than once before, the length of his fingers, browned by the sun and supple—not thickened and coarse like those of her father—hands better fitted for a pen of reed and scrolls of parchment than to guide a clumsy plow or gouge stones from a stubborn field.

"So much happened, and so strange"—at last Mark looked up to make slow answer—"I hardly have words to tell. I wish you had been there, Mary."

The little cloud, no bigger than the dark stone spindle where the thread was beginning to wind as she twisted the white wool from her distaff, scattered and dissolved in Mary's mind, the nameless apprehension melted away. For Mark had not left her out of his dreaming, he would not shut her away from his thinking. He wished she had been there— there in the shepherds' field, to follow the star with him.

"Were you able to catch up again with Jacob and Reuben?" she inquired, not so much pressing him to talk as to help him find a beginning.

"I met them turning back. Jacob, being old or else because the stones were too rough under foot, declared it was no great marvel anyhow, one beam more or less among so many in the heavens. And Reuben let himself be persuaded to give up."

No need to question whether Mark had given up, Mary thought with a swift rush of affection and pride, noting the taut thrust of squared shoulders under the coarse brown tunic, the purposeful lift of the head, dark against the whitewashed wall as the wing of a young raven. You had only to see Mark to know that whatever he undertook, he would keep on to the very end.

47

"Was it far to go?" she asked. "And did you arrive in good time?"

"As far as Bethlehem," he said simply. "And though I came late, I was yet in good time."

She waited for him to explain.

"Others had seen the star when first it appeared in the heavens, some twelve nights earlier—shepherds who had been abiding with their flock in a field near Bethlehem. When I came to the inn I found them gathered there—as each night since the birth of the child they had gathered to worship at the manger where the infant lay cradled."

Whether it was Mark's words or what Mary read into them, unspoken, of wonderment and mystery, a kind of Sabbath hush seemed to fall upon the room as when in the bare little synagogue on the windy hill the old rabbi lifted his hands to call down a blessing upon the waiting congregation. Mary laid her distaff aside to sit with hands folded in her lap, slim and tall, her eyes upon Mark, herself forgotten in her amazedness at him and the strangeness of the story he had to tell. For he seemed no longer a boy but a man, and the things of which he spoke were wondrous to hear.

A certain Joseph had journeyed from Nazareth to Bethlehem with his wife to be taxed according to the law of Caesar Augustus, Mark said, arranging in orderly sequence for Mary's better understanding such facts as he had learned from the shepherds, together with what he himself had later witnessed. For Joseph, so Mark had learned, was of the house and lineage of David, and Bethlehem, as everyone knows, is the city of David.

There in Bethlehem a child had been born that night to Mary, Joseph's young wife. And because there was no room for them at the inn, crowded as it was with those who had come from afar to pay their taxes, the child was wrapped in swaddling clothes and laid in a manger.

Mary . . . It was her own name, the very sound of it drew her toward that other Mary. Yet there was in the sound a difference too, as if the name were no longer plain and common for everyday use, but fresh and fair to make beautiful the verse of a psalmist. *Mary* . . .

Then, with the room so quiet that the rustling whisper of wood taking gradual fire from the ashes on the hearth was plain to hear, Mark went on to relate how an angel had come upon those other shepherds keeping watch over their flock in a field near Bethlehem, and the glory of the Lord had shone round them. They had been sore afraid, the shepherds, until the angel spoke.

"Fear not," the angel had said, "for behold, I bring you tidings of great joy, which shall be unto all people. For unto you is born this day in the city of David a Saviour, which is Christ the Lord. And this shall be a sign unto you: Ye shall find the babe wrapped in swaddling clothes, lying in a manger."

And suddenly—so the shepherds had told Mark, describing to him the marvelous event—suddenly there was with the angel a multitude of the heavenly host praising God and saying, "Glory to God in the highest, and on earth peace, good will toward men."

And after the angels had gone away into heaven, the shepherds went in great haste to Bethlehem, where they found the babe lying in a manger, just as the angel had said, and Mary his mother, and Joseph.

The picture was so clear in Mary's mind, so luminous with gentle light, it seemed more real than the rough-plastered walls of the room where she sat. She saw in imagination the kneeling figures of the shepherds, darkly shadowed against the earthen floor, saw within the circle of flickering lantern light the child in his swaddling clothes cradled in the hay, and seated on a bench beside the manger his fair young mother gazing down upon him, such an expression upon her face of awe and joy as though she were hearing still the echo of angel voices.

"I myself saw the three stranger wise men when they came," Mark was saying. "They had beheld his star in the East and came to worship him. For thus it had long ago been foretold by the prophet, that in Bethlehem the city of David a child should be born King of the Jews.

"Who the three strangers were and whence they had come I know not. Some took them to be magi out of the land of Chaldea, for the Chaldeans have always been wiser than other men in the knowledge of stars, and some would have it that they were kings or princes. But when they were come where the child lay in the manger they fell down and worshiped, and proffered him gifts out of their treasures—gold and frankincense and myrrh."

Magi . . . princes . . . kings. As plain to Mary's inner vision as Mark's earnest, sun-browned face fronting her across the smooth-scrubbed, bare table, she pictured the strange midnight scene—the three magi kings upon their knees before the child, their robes crowding with rich color the dark earthen floor, the wondering shepherds drawing aside to make room, and from the outer darkness looking on, the patient ox and mild-eyed donkey. The heads of the magi were bowed, their faces indistinct in the shadow, but the lantern light gleamed upon their hands outstretched with the offerings they had brought to the new-born king, the gold, the frankincense, the myrrh.

A gust of wind rattled at the loosely latched door and puffed down the chimney to scatter a gray cloud of ashes across the floor. A passing dog barked and in the adjoining room the goat resumed its restless pawing. And suddenly, with the homely sounds, all was turned familiar again, the four whitewashed walls, the shelf with the clay cooking vessels, Mark's broad-shouldered figure across the table.

Vanished were the magi, unknown, into the night out of which they had come. Quenched was the star, spent was the lantern shining down upon the child and his mother. Yet something of radiance seemed still to linger in the room— warming the walls to unaccustomed beauty and deepening the glow of firewood coals upon the gray hearth.

V

A DECISION

Feeling Mark's gaze upon her, Mary roused herself to speak. "And you," she said, "what do you think? Is it true as the magi said, that the child is king?"

But she knew it was. She could not reason it out or explain it, but she was as certain of it as that she was herself, alive and warm and breathing.

"He is a babe and helpless, Mary," Mark gravely reminded her. "He will have need of loyal men when he begins his rule. Yes, many are needed even now to help prepare the land for his reign." This was no dreaming youth who spoke, but one who had come young and strong to manhood. "All the long miles from Bethlehem I have been thinking about it, turning the matter over in my mind, trying to see how best I can serve."

Mary's pulse quickened. Nowhere in all Palestine would the king find another so loyal as Mark, hardy and brave and true. "You will be his scribe"—quick color flushed her cheeks, her eyes were shining—"and write his letters for him and keep tally of his treasury, and he will trust you with the secrets of his kingdom."

"You do not understand, Mary, you think like a girl of

glory and fame. How should anyone poor and ignorant as I become scribe to a king?"

He spoke sharply, impatient not with her but of how difficult it was going to be—almost impossible, perhaps—to make her understand the change which had come over his thinking. The experience of the past night, of awe and mystery, dwelt with him still. By its light his earlier ambition showed trivial and empty, no more than a boyish desire for honor and acclaim. Whether it had been the radiance that shone about the child in the manger, or the star-led magi kneeling in humble worship, or whether it was Mark's own thought reaching out to grasp what this might mean, it was as though he had glimpsed—felt rather than seen—some eternal purpose toward which the world was moving, half in darkness, and knew himself to share in that great purpose.

"Herod may be angered when he hears that another is to be king." Mark chose his words with care, hoping to make plain to Mary what he himself scarcely understood, by what reasoning as he traversed the chill, thorn-grown miles from Bethlehem, he had come to conceive for himself a goal so changed. "Herod is a covetous king, and cruel, with armies of soldiers at his command. The young king must have friends to shield and protect him.

"And even if Herod should be willing to yield the throne, the new-born king cannot unaided bring peace and good will to all in the land. He needs many to help him. It is not solely the yoke of our Roman masters which weighs upon us—the thought is not new with me, Mary, you yourself have often heard the rabbi exhort the congregation—but our own failings and wrongdoings.

"Why can we not learn to dwell in brotherly kindness together?" It might have been himself Mark was reproaching for some failure of responsibility, he spoke so low. "There are men imprisoned whom nobody remembers, and blind men and crippled, and men who hunger and have no bread. Often in the stillness of the night keeping watch over the flock, I think of them, or by day in the green pastures, wondering how such men live.

"And there are those enslaved, bound to endless toil in reeking dye-factories and the flaming furnaces where they make brick, or chained to Roman galleys. My own thought speaks to tell me my place is there among them, and what I can do, that I must." His eyes pled with her to strengthen him in his difficult resolve, but she was not looking. "Do you comprehend, Mary?"

Comprehend—did she comprehend? The word echoed dully in her ear. Why did he ask? What difference would it make to him whether or not she comprehended? One thing alone of all he said was clear—he would forsake her, he had made his choice between her and the king.

She stared straight before her, unseeing. Did he take her for a child, she would like to ask him, for a weakly child that he must spin it out with many words and beat about the bush? Yes, she knew, if he should ask her again, she knew what it was he feared to say in plain sentences. He was putting her aside. She was to have no part in his life.

"Not as a scribe, not as one close to the king am I fitted to serve, Mary, but among the poor and the humble." Mark touched her sleeve to make her look at him, but she would not. "How should there be place for one like me at the court?"

She was not listening, she did not hear him. . . . The dreams they had dreamed of the future, the plans they had made, how he would study, turning over many books until he had mastered the world's wisdom, while she would keep the house for him and weave garments of fine scarlet for his wear when he went among the elders of the Temple—all this was as nothing, and she less than nothing to him now.

A sudden anger choked her, knotted in her chest, burned in her throat. Well, let him go! Why should she care? Let him forget her and follow the king. She would not care, it would not matter to her. Let him go wherever he would, why should he suppose it would matter to her?

"I do not know when I shall be able to come home again." What hardships might lie ahead, he could not measure. "Or how I shall find employment—I a shepherd and Tyre so vast a city, with so many dark alleys of close-crowded hovels. The rabbi says that while the great ones revel and waste, the poor go hungry."

The words went past Mary, only one caught her attention. "Tyre?" As well say the other side of the world, it was so far beyond hope of return. "What of Jerusalem?" By a great effort she kept her voice level.

"Jerusalem is Herod's city. To speak there of a new king would be sedition. No, it is not yet the time for Jerusalem."

Mark did not intend to return. She had known it all along, ever since he first started talking of the new king; he meant never to see her again. The hot color ebbed from her cheeks, her breath caught in her throat, and only her pride held back the tears that ached beneath her eyelids.

"I am not asking you to wait, Mary, it would not be fair, with nothing to offer, but if—" the sentence stumbled, hope floundering in doubt—"I mean, if you were still here and—"

"Oh, didn't you know?" She interrupted him with a stiff little laugh, rising abruptly to busy herself at the fire. "I shall soon be going away." She kept her head turned lest her eyes betray her with their wretchedness.

He assumed that Simon had given consent for her to seek employment in some household of wealth in Bethlehem or Gibeah. "But those places are at no great distance," he observed, relieved to think it.

"Who said that was where I shall go?" Her pride flared up that he should receive her announcement with so little show of concern. Again the little stilted laugh. She must not let him think she cared. "You've used up two of your guesses. Try again."

Then, before there was time for him to speak, she heard herself say, "But you'd never guess—I've decided after all to go to Pompeii." And having said it, she felt a wild hope spring up within her that Mark would not let her, that he would plead with her to go with him to Tyre instead.

For they were not bound by any bonds, they were not betrothed, there was no more than an understanding between their two fathers. And it might be that with Mark long absent and she with no clear promise of his return, her father would wish to betroth her to another. Or what if—swift fear barbed her thought—what if some Tyrian girl should find favor in Mark's sight? For the women of Tyre were said to be fairer than elsewhere in the land, fair as enchantresses in their bright silken gowns.

"Pompeii!" Mark was shocked. "To live in pagan Italy among the Gentiles and work for the Roman oppressors?" He mustered stern arguments to convict her of her own unreasoning folly (the rabbi himself could scarcely have argued better), reminded her of the prediction that at the day of judgment the Romans would burn like stubble in the fire, pointed out Pompeii's ill reputation as a city of wealth and temptation, and appealed to her conscience to consider her duty to her father.

"It is the duty of Miriam to keep the house for my father." Mark might as well have reasoned with the fire smoldering beneath the ashes on the hearth.

"And as for working for the Romans," Mary demanded, hurt and indignant that Mark should presume to rebuke her, "what is so wrong about that, I'd like to know? Half the people of Judea have been in their employ."

In the end Mark gave up the attempt to dissuade her, seeing that she would not listen to reason. "If I knew any argument that would make you change your mind—" he said heavily, gathering up his shepherd's staff. "But I've said all I know to say. We must not quarrel, it would only hurt us both. Because I must set forth for Tyre on the morrow, Mary. My work lies there, and the roads are slow of travel now in the season of snows and rains."

Watching in silence as he threw his brown patched cloak over his shoulder, his expression fixed and unsmiling, Mary felt her hope break apart within her. It had been her wounded pride which had seized upon Pompeii. The threat had failed, she had been mistaken. Mark did not love her. He did not need her.

She would have spoken as he went out the door, some casual word of friendly goodbye to show that this parting was no different from any other, but her lips were stiff and would not shape the words.

Numbly she fitted the lid to the stone fruit jar to stow it in the dark cranny in the inner wall, and brushed the crumbs of cheese from the table into her open palm, and poured water from the pitcher to rinse Mark's cup before she set it back in place upon the shelf. There was something else she had to do—the bread. She must not keep the baker waiting.

Nevertheless she did not hasten, smoothing her hair with a wooden comb and shaking the wrinkles from her cloak and washing her hands a second time. Nobody must have occasion to whisper behind her back that she looked dejected and mopish, and could there have been a falling out betwixt her and Mark? Because she was not in the least dejected, she told herself valiantly, summoning her pride to scoff at such weakness. It had been enough to make anybody lose her temper, the uppity way Mark had preached at her, though fortunately she had managed to hold her tongue.

She would put him out of her mind altogether. Now that she had discovered how he put his own desires ahead of hers, she could stop bothering about him and go her own way. She had only to make up her mind to it and he would be as good as forgotten. The very idea of his lecturing her about Pompeii as though she had no mind of her own! She would go where she wanted to, she assured herself obstinately, to put down the chill loneliness that crept about her heart.

By the time Mary had reached the lower end of the street she had argued herself into believing that she was determined to go to Pompeii. To live among the Romans would be an adventure, and why shouldn't she venture? She would be earning money too, which should carry weight with her father, as cash was scarce in a country poor as Judea. Nor would she be long absent, not more than a year or two at most, until the little lame boy grew bigger.

Perhaps it was an unacknowledged, hardly formulated hope that another year or two might see Mark returning from Tyre to claim her, or it might have been her own stubborn will warming to her purpose, or the gusts of wintry wind that brought the color to her face and quickened her step. Whatever the cause, the leaden weight that had

numbed and unnerved her was lifting, and she was beginning to feel, if not less unhappy, certainly less utterly helpless and forlorn.

The three or four dark-shawled women waiting their turn
at the oven made room for her in an angle of the wall, sheltered from the wind. "The air is raw," said one, "it's blowing
up to rain again." And another remarked that Simon and
Miriam had done well to get an early start. Had Mary heard
Simon express an opinion as to whether the tax would go
higher this year?

"Twice taxed we are," a toothless old woman mumbled,
grudgingly yielding up a rusted bronze coin at the baker's

demand. "First the Roman publicans rob us, and what's left our own priests take from us for the Temple. Aye, when it comes to taxes," she glowered at the baker as though his were the blame, "one's as bad as t'other, publican or priest."

At which the other women made mouths behind her back, knowing how often she had wheedled the rabbi out of his just due with one whining excuse or another. But they did not hold it too much against her, since she was old and money was hard to come by. And when she went stumping off with her fresh-baked loaf of barley bread, the flat round rolled loosely like a scroll for easier carrying under her shawl, they called out a "Good day and good appetite" after her retreating back as kindly as to any other.

Two or three children appeared, balancing upon their heads the wooden bowls their mothers had filled with balls of dough, and one little girl, racing to be first, spilled hers and the dough balls went scattering among the ruts in the stony street.

"No harm's done," Mary proclaimed, quick to make light of the accident before the child could screw up her face to weep. "Just look how clean they brush off! Aren't you the lucky girl it's the season of rains and the street's washed clean?" She made it seem so eventful the others almost wished they had spilled their bowls too, to have Mary pay attention to them.

Restless and chafing, she welcomed the slight diversion. For some reason, she did not know why, the whole village seemed overnight to have turned humdrum and cheerless, with nothing to look forward to, day after day always the same. Obed the baker, dark browed and gaunt in his patched tunic, humped on a stool beside the low stone oven, didn't he ever get tired of what he was doing? Feeding the fire a handful of sticks to heat the flat baking stone, pulling and stretching at a ball of dough and patting it parchment thin on his wooden tray, his eyes smarting with smoke and reddened from peering under the rounded stone hood of the oven to make sure the loaf was baked through before he hauled it out with his long, iron-pronged stick—didn't he ever rebel and want to run away and try something different?

Yes, the more she thought about it, the gladder she was that she would not have to stay on here forever, growing wrinkled and old and maybe having to live all alone like old Esther. Yes, she was glad she had made up her mind to go to Pompeii.

If it occurred to Mary how little of joy there was in her gladness, she pushed the thought aside.

VI

THE JOURNEY BEGINS

"For you the journeying will be new, Mary," Lollia turned half round on her donkey to observe, with a brisk slap of her poplar switch to spur the creature to mend its lagging gait, "but for me that's accustomed to Roman comfort, I'd liefer be sentenced to the mill to turn the wheel with slaves.

"Except for my little Rufus, I'd have feigned the falling sickness, never to set foot outside of Pompeii. But for you, I say," she hastened to repeat, struck by a canny thought she could not afford to paint too dark a picture of the inconveniences of travel lest Mary be moved to change her mind and face about homeward while yet there was time, "for you it will be all pleasure.

"You are young, your bones slide smooth as oiled wheels of a new-built chariot. Aye, my girl, wait till you're my age"—Lollia's apple-red cheeks, the liveliness of her movements, cast considerable doubt upon the various aches and ailments to which she made frequent claim—"at my age you'll learn soon enough what it is to have your joints creak and groan like a worn-out wine-press."

A company of four, Lollia, Mary, the two legionaries Julius and Cato, they had just left the town of Gibeah behind on their way to join Sextus and his train some miles further on. The sun was slanting toward the west, the season of rains was almost at end, the hillsides were sheathed in new green, patched bright with wildflowers. Poppies and anemones laced with scarlet the thin fields of barley and rye, wild geraniums gave back the blue of the sky, and here and there a late asphodel, not yet withered on its stalk, swayed soft grayish pink among the rockroses and pale yellow of slender-stemmed scabiouses. Even the rusty thornbushes were budding green, and in the air above the hawk seemed to glide on wings of sun.

It was a day so filled with sun and the freshness and stir of springtime that there was no room left for misgivings and regret. The homesickness was lifting that through the morning hours had weighed upon Mary's mind with sorrow of parting and half dread of the new world she was about to enter, of tempting and threatening things. Never before had she traveled farther than Bethlehem or Gibeah, and that but seldom, and now with every bend in the narrow road she gazed more eagerly about her.

And when a ragged, half-grown goatherd lolling in the shade of a wild fig tree sent his black- and brown-speckled flock hastily scrabbling down the steep bank out of the way of the soldiers, but himself lingered at the road's rim to follow the little procession enviously with his eyes, Mary felt a sudden exhilaration. For it was she that the boy was envying, she riding out from the hills that ringed Judea like a wall. This was she who was adventuring out into the great world where wide-built cities stood beside the sea, and cara-vans and pack trains and chariots daily came and went, and the Leviathan made his lair fathoms deep beneath the wa-tery ocean floor. Had ever a girl before in all Palestine been so lucky! and daring too—and certain to succeed!

"Not till the lord Sextus and master Rufus have been served their supper will I present you for their approval," Lollia turned again somewhat later to shout over her shoul-der. Talk was difficult, what with the soldiers lengthening their stride not to have darkness overtake them, and the lurching see-saw of Mary's and Lollia's donkeys on the downhill grade.

"Men folk are better dispositioned after they've been fed," Lollia lifted her voice to explain above the clop-clop of hoofs and scrunch of sliding pebbles. "Besides, it'll give you time to get into your other dress, and I'll give you a ribbon to bind your hair." She was desirous on her own account that Mary should make a good impression. "The lord Sextus likes his servitors genteel of garb, as befits a quaestor of Caesar Augustus."

Mary had intended to save for Pompeii her Sabbath dress —brown-dyed, with a border of red and a scarlet sash—but she nodded to show her willingness to be guided by Lollia's advice. An hour's extra wearing would not make the gar-ment look less new, provided she could keep the little boy from putting sticky hands to it.

It was not yet dusk when they arrived at the stream where Sextus' train had struck camp, some twenty or thirty

65

soldiers, as many servants, several civilian officers, assistants
to the quaestor, and riding horses, dogs, and a score or
more of pack-asses. A pair of tents had already been set up
on a level plot above the stream, and pegs were being driven
for a third.

"That's for the women," Lollia pointed Mary to the
smaller of the tents. "If anyone questions, tell 'em I sent
you. It'll be nobody but one of the young master's serving
women, or maybe the new wife the steward got himself in
Sidon. I'm off to see how the young master fared today
without his old nurse, to ready him for his supper."

As Mary stooped to lift the tent flap, one or two of the
women eyed her curiously and one nodded a greeting, but
the others kept on with what they were doing, indifferent
to her presence. The light was dim, the tent small and
crowded. At one side two women were fitting together the
wooden frame of a child's cot and another was spreading
straw and blankets for pallets, while still another unpacked
the contents of a dust-stained saddlebag—a child's tunic
and cloak and sandals, some wooden toys, a small metal cup
with a rounded handle.

At the rear of the tent a woman sat preening herself before a bronze hand mirror she had propped upon a pair of
saddlebags, though Mary wondered how in so dim a light
she could see. Mary would have liked to approach nearer
to observe more closely, for she had often heard how Roman
ladies—and some of the fine ladies of Jerusalem too—painted
their faces to make themselves appear bright of color as

statues. It must be she who was wife to the steward, she seemed to have no work to do and was so much younger than the others.

The straw pallets were being spread closer to Mary's feet, one of the women dragged another set of saddlebags into the tent to unpack, and still nobody took any particular notice of Mary. Perhaps it was because they were Roman and she was not, she thought, or it might be that in the dim light they took her to be one of them. Anyhow, with the tent so crowded it might be better to wait outside. She would find a sheltered place along the stream to wash her hands and face and comb her hair and lave her feet and wipe her sandals clean of dust.

She skirted the tethered pack-asses braying to be fed and watered, made a wide circuit to avoid a group of soldiers dicing beneath a sycamore tree, and following upward along the narrow, rocky watercourse came to a clump of oleander bushes overhanging the stream. A kingfisher dived for his supper, and a jay flitted from stem to stem of the oleander to scold at her, his plumage bold black and white among the green foliage.

The water was cold, the current swift where she waded in, lifting her long skirts to keep them from being draggled. She stood for a moment to feel the water swirl fresh and clean about her ankles, the breeze cool against her face. She was drying her feet with a bunch of grass when a sound of sobbing caught her ear—a child lost or in trouble somewhere farther along the bank to her left.

"I'm coming," she called, clambering hastily down to the stream again, and then because it might be a Roman child, changed the Aramaic tongue to the Latin, "Wait—I'm coming!"

A minute or two later she spied the child among the rocks at the water's edge. At first she thought he must have stumbled and fallen, and then she saw that he was attempting to get at some object which bobbed up and down just beyond his reach where a fall of gravel had trapped the water in an eddying pool.

At sight of her he redoubled his wails, his face so red with temper and streaked with tears he might have been weeping for hours instead of minutes. "He falled in," he greeted her with a sob, rubbing his eyes with the back of a grimy little fist, "Cwocky falled in."

"Naughty bad Crocky!" Mary drew her brows together in a frown, sternly disapproving such unseemly behavior on the part of the wooden toy she glimpsed rocking idly up and down upon the water. "We'll find a stick and pull him safe back to shore," she promised cheerily, giving a hand to the child to help him up.

His tunic was wet and dirty, his hair tousled, his knees scratched where he must have bumped them against a ledge. "Find 'tick," he echoed, his face brightening. He was quick of movement and sturdy, with a broad forehead and light blue eyes, and his damp small hand rested trustingly in hers.

" 'Tick for Cwocky"—a smile was breaking through, and

he gave a little hop to show how ready he was—"find 'tick." She noticed then that he was lame, dragging one foot. Could it be that he was Lollia's little Rufus?

But the sticks they found were mere twigs and the oleander bushes too tough to yield to Mary's tugging. Rather than disappoint the child she must wade into the water again, though it was deeper here and the sun was sinking and she ought to take the little boy back where he came from before anyone began to worry. And whatever would Lollia think if she returned to find Mary missing?

She had just stepped out of the water, dripping toy crocodile in hand—wouldn't baby Saul crow with delight at so astonishing a plaything, long-tailed and green-painted with a deep red mouth that opened and closed as you pulled a string—and was stooping to squeeze the water from the hems of her skirt when someone spoke. "What's going on here?"

It was a tall, sandy-haired legionary in a white tunic, or at least she supposed from the short-sword sheathed in bronze at his belt that he was a soldier, an officer, she thought, perhaps a centurion, since he wore a gold ring about his arm and a gold chain about his neck. How long he had been standing there in the shadow of the boulder she had no way of knowing. Not long, she hoped. It was embarrassing to think he might have been watching her.

"The little boy's toy fell into the water." She could feel the red color mantling her face. "Don't punish him," she pleaded as he hoisted the child summarily upon his shoulder.

Soldiers had a reputation for roughness, and this one was unsmiling. "He didn't mean to run away, he's hardly more than a baby."

The centurion made no reply—maybe he had not heard her—but Mary thought from the accustomed way the child hooked an arm about the man's neck that they must be acquainted. If the boy was Lollia's little Rufus—and he must be, since they had sent so imposing an officer in search of him—why, then she need not worry that he wouldn't be well treated.

It was growing dusk when Lollia returned to the tent. "Young master's been lost, the men folk were slack in their care of him," she announced with relish for all the tent to hear. Lollia had no high opinion of the dependability of the opposite sex, perhaps because she had in her time been nurse to too many a helter-skelter small boy.

"Worn to a frazzle I am, with the search and the worry!" Had Mary not known, she might have given Lollia full credit for finding the child, she sounded so self-important. "And drenched to the skin I am besides, the restless way the lad threshed about when I tried to wash the mud off him. The master's too busy to see you now, Mary. You must wait till the morrow or the next day.

"You, Claudia," Lollia addressed one of the serving women, "why haven't you and the others gone to fetch supper? I declare," she grumbled, lifting a little clay lamp to peer among the piled saddlebags to see which was hers, "sometimes I think I'm the only one with a head on her shoulders. Hurry now, before the soldiers fish all the mutton out of the cauldrons and nothing's left but shreds of garlic and blobs of barley.

"And look to it that Haephestium doesn't put a piece that's all gristle and bone on my charger," she poked her head through the tent to call after Mary. "Tell him to give me some morsels of marrow-fat too, to spread on my bread for breakfast, to make it go down easy."

"Sets herself up as better 'n the rest of us," one of the servants muttered in Mary's ear, but Mary pretended not to understand. "You'd think she was the lady Livia herself, the airs she puts on." Getting no response from Mary, the serving woman sought other company.

Why it was as Mary stood lonesome and quiet among the half dozen middle-aged women waiting their turn at the steaming cauldrons, a great longing for home should unexpectedly come upon her, she could not have told. She was not even thinking about the baby Saul or her father, but there they suddenly were—the baby stretching out his arms to be taken and her father swinging him up into the air, squealing and kicking out helplessly with delight.

For a moment only the picture in her mind was real. All else seemed insubstantial as shadow, the tongues of fire licking at the blackened cauldrons, the soldiers jostling and joking as they fell into line with their empty wooden chargers, the tethered pack-asses cropping the thin grass by the roadside, the hills darkly irregular against the fading sunset sky.

And still, an hour or two later, as she drew up a blanket

on the pallet beside Lollia, still the homesickness blurred her thought so that she hardly knew whether to be glad or sorry she was adventuring out into the great world. When she fell asleep, it was to dream of the steep home pasture and the sheep grazing white among the gray rocks and Mark laughing at the odd-sounding Roman word he was reading from the rabbi's scroll. Mary laughed too, for the word was *crocodilus*.

Sextus' train was early under way the next morning, the tents and other gear tied on pack-asses, Sextus and his officers in the lead on sleek, high-stepping horses. Mary caught an occasional glimpse of them far ahead in the narrow valley as her donkey rounded a curve on the trail—and after them a file of legionaries briskly marching, and then the women on donkeys, serving men leading the pack animals in irregular procession, and more soldiers with iron spears and short-swords, for the roads were infested with robbers.

Rufus was riding with his father, having spent the night in his father's tent. Later, when Sextus had to take count of a village treasury and question the publican, the child would bide with Lollia and Mary. Two brawny serving men carried a litter ready for his greater comfort when he grew weary, and Lollia had honey cakes and the toy crocodile in her wallet to soothe him when he fretted.

"No wonder the child is sometimes peevish and unruly, having to be everlastingly on the move. If it were anybody else but the lady Livia was his mother, though I say it as I shouldn't—

"Stop it there, Haephestium," she interrupted herself to shout at the cook, her voice shrill with vexation. "Can't you look where you're going?" She struck at his donkey with her poplar switch as Haephestium and his helpers came crowding by to take their places near the head of the line. "Have you no eyes in your head to see who it is you're pushing off the path?"

The dogs frisked and barked, the bronze cooking vessels clanged noisily together as the donkeys trotted past, but Haephestium, Mary noticed with a grin to think how wasted was old Lollia's wrath, rode with his eyes closed, his shaven head nodding, heavy with sleep. He was a short fat man, round as a wine cask, and it must have been a relief to him to be able to rest his feet.

"Nor don't you go lauding the waters of Callirrhoë to me, my girl, because I know better." Lollia hardly waited for the dust and the din to subside to pronounce a solemn warning, as though Mary had mentioned the subject. "As for curing the child, he might as well have been dipped in goat's milk. A penny a glass they charged for it too, the black-bearded swindlers!

"Quarts of it his father made him drink, till the child turned green-sickish to smell the bitter smell, poor little innocent." It required no more from Mary than a quick nod now and then, or an appropriately sympathetic shake of the head or rounding of lips into an O of surprise, to keep Lollia's tongue wagging.

As nurse to the young master she held herself superior

to common serving women, although when other audience lacked she was not above stooping to their company; but with Mary it was different. She herself had selected Mary, the young master had been pleased to let Mary assist with his dressing and feeding when Sextus' man servant carried him to their tent at dawn, and she had no doubt that when the lord Sextus found time for it he would commend Lollia for her choice of helper.

Not that Lollia had any intention of letting the girl get an exaggerated notion of her own importance. There was no reason, however, why she should not treat her as an equal, provided of course that Mary did not overstep or fail in deference. And Lollia flattered herself that Mary was too well aware of all she was owing to Lollia to try to take advantage of her, like the young upstart they had left behind in Sidon.

Several days elapsed before Lollia could present Mary for Sextus' approval, and then the opportunity came by chance. The train had encamped somewhat earlier in the afternoon than usual, just beyond the gate of a stone- and mud-walled village. While they waited for their tent to be set up and the saddlebags brought, Lollia and Mary strolled with Rufus down the rocky slope to where the village spring welled cool and dark at the root of a wide-spreading sycamore tree.

A rounded wall of roughly smoothed stone prevented the water from wasting, and the steps leading down to it were blackened and slippery with damp so that Mary had to hold Rufus by the hand to keep him from falling. After she had

74

given him to drink from the leather cup in her wallet and twice carried the cup up the steps to quench Lollia's thirst, then the crocodile must have its turn.

"Not here, Crocky says, please not here," Mary persuaded the little boy, since at any minute Haephestium's half dozen dark-skinned Egyptian scullery boys might come clattering with kettles and pots and great leather bags to fill in haste to start the supper cooking.

"Crocky wants to play in the sun and snap at gnats." She pitched her voice to a squeaky falsetto, a version of crocodile accents which served as well as any, since Rufus knew no more than she what kind of voice a crocodile might speak with.

It was not Haephestium's noisy scullions, however, whom Mary almost bumped head into as she helped Rufus mount the last steep, slimy step to the flat stone where Lollia stood waiting in the rustling green shade of the sycamore, but a tall soldier in a purple-bordered tunic. "The lord Sextus would speak with you, Mary," Lollia greeted her, somewhat flustered and red of face, anxious that at this unexpected meeting with the quaestor Mary should make a good impression.

Because if Sextus thought Mary looked too young and flighty—and he well might think it, the unruly way her hair was blowing in damp tendrils across her forehead, and her eyes so sparkling blue with laughter at some joke she must have been playing with the child—Sextus might yet refuse to keep her in his employ. For he was most particular

75

about those who served his little son. Of course it was to his credit that he should be so, but there was no denying it was sometimes a trial to Lollia, having already cost her the loss of two likely young helpers before ever they had departed from Italy. And where could she find another so to her liking if Sextus should choose to send Mary packing?

Mary, for her part, was so astonished at sight of the soldier —and even more amazed to see that it was the same sandy-haired, gold-braceleted officer who had come in search of the strayed Rufus on that first evening of her journey—that it was two or three seconds before she quite realized that this, then, could be no other than the mighty lord Sextus himself, quaestor of the emperor Augustus.

Not until another couple of seconds had passed did she remember to drop down upon one knee, as Lollia had previously instructed her, and bow her head humbly according to the Roman custom until Sextus should bid her rise. She did not feel in the least humble, but curious and excited and at the same time rather uncomfortably self-conscious, wishing her hair were combed smooth and the dust shaken from her dress.

Strangely though, kneeling there, waiting for Sextus to speak, she felt something almost like shame tighten her temples and flush her cheeks with burning red to think that she, one of God's free people, should bow thus low to a worshiper of Roman idols. But it was only for manners' sake she was doing it, she assured herself on the instant, shoving the uncomfortable thought out of sight. If she intended to dwell

among Romans, she must learn to practice Roman customs.

"Lollia tells me that you are willing to come to Pompeii, Mary, to give assistance with the child." Sextus touched her upon the shoulder, bidding her stand.

"Yes, sir." Mary's voice was low, her face scarlet, but she held herself proudly.

His eyes took measure of her as though it were the first time he had seen her—grave gray eyes, summing her carefully and passing judgment. "Lollia will instruct you in your duties," he said, and that was all. He looked down briefly to admire the shiny pebble Rufus held up for him to see and then went striding off up the slope to the village.

"There, Mary, you see for yourself how the master relies upon my judgment." Lollia hardly waited until he was out of earshot to plume herself upon the successful outcome of the encounter. "Next time you must wear the dress with the sash, to put a better foot forward." Lollia was partial to bright colors.

Before Rufus had tired of piling up twigs for a house for Crocky, they had to run to the tent to escape a drenching from a cloud that sprang up with a wind from nowhere, spattering the dust with great round drops and twanging through the leaves of the sycamore like a thousand-stringed silver lyre. The shower lasted but minutes, the season of rains being almost at end, and when the sun appeared again the herd boys came driving the goats through the lengthening shadows to be milked outside the village gate.

It was the hour of day when women were passing back

and forth through the gate in the thick white-washed wall with earthen water jars upon their shoulders to fill at the spring, chatting and laughing together as they came and went. It was all so familiar, the dark-haired women with their smooth-curving clay jars, the threads of white smoke beginning to rise above the wall as hearths were lighted, the homely smells of appetizing stews, barley and lentil, garlic-flavored, warming for supper, and the low, lingering voice of the breeze passing over, that for a minute Mary was homesick and envious.

"You're lucky," she had to remind herself sharply. "Would you remain always in the same one place, afraid to venture?"

She bought goat's milk in a leather bowl for Rufus and paid for it with the penny Lollia had given her, and when he had drunk it set him astraddle the pet brown goat which a smiling bare-legged herd boy led up beside them.

The name of the village was Tappuah, the boy told Mary, and it was in the land of Samaria. A little farther on there would be a dividing of the way, one fork leading westward to Caesarea and the ocean and the other following northward through the town of Nazareth and past the Sea of Galilee till it came at last to the city of Tyre. Whence had Mary come, and whither was she bound?

Although the boy's age could not have been more than twelve, he spoke with such assurance of alien cities and distant seas that Mary felt ashamed to be so ignorant. How could it be possible, she longed to know but feared to inquire lest he laugh at her lack of knowledge, and she so much older than he—how could it possibly be that no matter whether you traveled with the caravan trail to the west or to the north you would come equally to the ocean? It didn't make sense that it could be in two different places at once.

One question, however, she must put to the boy, it had for so many days occupied her mind. Was it from Caesarea or from Tyre that the Roman ships set sail for Pompeii? Once Lollia had told her Caesarea and another time Tyre, and yesterday she had said what difference did it make, one place was as good as another and whichever it was the lord Sextus would see to everything, Mary needn't fret herself, the donkeys would get them there in plenty of time.

But it did make a difference which city it was, as Mary might have explained to Lollia, except that not even to her inmost self would she have been willing to acknowledge the secret dream upon which her hope fed—that she would find Mark waiting for her there at the gates of Tyre where he was serving the new-born king.

So now, "From which city do the Roman ships sail?" she inquired of the boy, tightening her grip to hold Rufus from falling as the herd boy took the goat by its two stubby horns to lead toward the low stone trough where Lollia, with gesture and pantomime, was engaged in sprightly communication with two old women who were grinding barley for bread.

"Depends upon the cargo," the boy was pleased to inform Mary, displaying the large knowledge he had picked up from drivers of passing caravans. "Caesarea or Tyre or Sidon, the Roman triremes put in at 'em all. Sidon's where the glassworks are. I know, 'cause a Tappuah man's gone there to work for the Romans."

VII

ON THE WAY

As THE journey lengthened, the wife of the steward became friendly with Mary. Lodged in the tent with the serving women, her husband twice her age and continually busied with his account books and the checking of supplies and gear for Sextus, she was often bored and restless. Like Mary, she was fond of children, and like Mary, she was young. But there the resemblance ended.

Her name was Phyllis and she was Greek, her father a prosperous grain merchant of Sidon, and her casual talk of city life stirred Mary to marvel at houses with baths of marble and rooms with walls of azure-colored plaster or rosy-red or yellow, whose floors bore pictures of birds and beasts and gods, all made of flat, smooth-polished stones no bigger than your fingernail, set cunningly together.

Although it was undeniably flattering to have Phyllis seek her company, Mary was more grateful than flattered. She too was sometimes homesick, she too wished for a companion of her own age. Nor was it only Phyllis' nimble chatter of shops and clothes, of weddings and festivals with processions by torchlight, that kept Mary endlessly interested, nor the dresses Phyllis wore—bright wool, downy to touch as breasts of doves, or silky Egyptian cotton, according to the weather—which so attracted Mary.

There was something about her very person, softly plump and small, the black hair arrayed in crisp ringlets to fringe the low forehead and rounded oval of her cheeks, the long ends gathered into a knot at the nape of her neck, the darkness of her eyes exaggerated by the lines she drew with a practiced hand to lengthen her eyebrows—some mixture of sooty black and scented balm—which Mary found entrancing. And Phyllis was sociable, not at all inclined to put on airs when she was alone with Mary and Rufus although she sometimes affected a more aristocratic manner than she had been born to, to impress the others.

"Put my toilet box there on the saddle-bag, Claudia," she directed the serving woman. "Next time see to it that your hands are clean before you touch it."

And to Mary, "Let the unpacking wait. There'll be time enough later, but what I must do must be done before set of sun." She was lifting the painted lid of a small teakwood toilet box as she spoke, to rummage hastily among the stoppered glass scent bottles and cosmetic jars. "Come, Mary"— extracting a scrap or two of ribbon from the box—"come, we must hurry."

Less than an hour earlier, Sextus' party had arrived at the caravansary in the hills not far from the Sea of Galilee near the town of Magdala, where the trail began to slant gradually westward on its way down toward the ocean. They were cramped for space, the great square enclosure being already crowded with two caravans bound for Egypt and a numerous train of pack-asses carrying cedar wood to the city of Tyre. But the camel men and the donkey men obligingly crowded their beasts closer together to make room, and Titus the steward, careful to dispose of Sextus' officials according to their rank, managed to find several cubicles vacant among those fronting the courtyard on the fourth side. He assigned to the women the one in the corner as safest, being farthest from the gate, although with so many armed legionaries in the train there was little likelihood that thieves would attempt to break in.

Hand in hand, their heads modestly covered, looking neither to right nor left, Mary and Phyllis hugged the wall of the great open-air inn as they passed through the courtyard on their way toward the massive wooden gate. Mary longed to linger to gaze her fill at the kneeling camels and fierce-looking turbaned men with knives in their belts who were freeing the beasts of the heavy bales and bags that swung from either side of their humps. For Sidon-born Phyllis caravans with men in outlandish garb from unknown lands were a commonplace, but for Mary who had dwelt all her life remote from any caravan route, the temptation to stare was hardly to be resisted.

Out of the corner of her eye she caught a tantalizing glimpse of a strange bright bird perched upon the shoulder of a black-bearded man in a white turban. To Mary's astonishment the bird was speaking words, though what their meaning might be she did not know. The man smiled to see with what curiosity she regarded the bird, but she quickly looked away, blushing and embarrassed.

"Quick, quick, before he puts the evil eye upon us!" Phyllis whispered, drawing her mantle across her face. "Make the sign— It's that dwarfish fellow there by the gate with the mules. Hold this to protect you till we pass him." She thrust a scrap of blue ribbon at Mary.

With forefinger and little finger straight outstretched, the shred of blue held in plain sight against her palm between her two infolded middle fingers and thumb, Mary hastily made the sign of the horns. For though there were some persons, Mark among them, who scoffed at the idea that anyone just by casting his eyes upon you could work his will upon you for evil, make you fall into an illness and perhaps die, there was no use in taking chances. And certainly the muleteer, now that Mary's attention had been called to him, was not one you would feel comfortable to have stare at you, a thick, squat fellow with a thatch of red hair and a long scar across his cheek, and only one eye.

Outside the gate, instead of heading toward the village as Mary had expected, Phyllis turned in the opposite direction, back along the trail by which they had come. Before there was time to inquire why they should walk away from Magdala instead of toward it to have a look around, Mary sensed the reason—sensed it in her dainty, comely friend with something of shock, as one discovers an imperfection in what had else appeared whole and perfect, without flaw or blemish.

A short distance above them on the hill a clump of thornbushes sprouted from the rocky ledge which marked the
boundary of a cultivated field. It was a barley field, almost
ready for reaping, but the yield would be scant for the soil
was thin and much grown with thistles and wild mustard.
A hawk screeched as it flew over, and a flight of eagles made
a swift-moving pattern high in the white of the air. But it

was none of these things, nor the marigolds carpeting with gold the terraced slopes that led irregularly up to the orchards of fig and olive and almond which attracted Mary's notice and gave her a clue to Phyllis' intent.

For it was upon the clump of thornbushes that Phyllis' eyes were bent, a scraggly growth in nowise different from thousands of others they had already passed, scattered across fields and hillsides, stubbornly rooted in barren, stony earth, except that from the branches of these particular shrubs there fluttered various bits of faded rag and scraps of cloth.

"The eagles are a good omen, did you notice?" Phyllis remarked. "There must be a special virtue in these bushes, that so many have made votive offering here. I've an extra piece of ribbon for you, Mary, in case you haven't any.

"Do you know what prayer I make whenever we pass a place like this?" She dropped her voice to a whisper as they approached the thorn, not to disturb whatever spirit, good or evil, might have chanced to take up its residence therein. "It's that when I have a baby son he won't walk lame like poor little Rufus.

"But of course what you want is a husband, Mary. That's why I brought a specially nice piece of blue for you—and besides, it's potent to ward off any evil powers that happen to be hanging around, trying to make trouble."

In Mary's own village there were persons who, although on the Sabbath day they worshiped in the synagogue like everybody else, would tell you in secret how you could obtain your dearest wish by whispering a prayer to the gnarled old terebinth tree that stood in the lee of the hill (to make sure that the tree remembered, you must tie a bit of yarn to one of the twigs), and how, if you would carry hidden under your clothes, wrapped in blue cloth, a lump of resin from that same tree, you never need fear black witch or demon.

Mostly they were stupid people who believed it, and Mary's grandmother had early set Mary's mind against such heathenish practices. Because as the rabbi said, what power had one stick or stone for good or ill more than any other? Never a Sabbath went by but that the rabbi reminded them that they were people chosen of God. How then could they put their trust in things of wood and stone or worship graven images as did the pagan Romans?

Mary was amazed, and troubled too, to think that Phyllis would kneel in petition to a barren thornbush, clever pretty Phyllis who knew such heaps of things Mary had never even heard about. "You mustn't," she protested. "It's nothing but a bush, it can't even hear what you're saying to it." (Had it been a terebinth tree, she thought, there might perhaps have been some excuse for Phyllis.) "Thornbushes are a pest, they grew from the tent pegs of the Philistines when David fought with Goliath."

Phyllis had never heard of David or Goliath. "If it's a demon inhabits the bush"—putting a finger to her lip to caution Mary to speak more softly—"then all the more reason to propitiate it."

That old Lollia should have faith in snakeskins and amulets and say prayers to clay images that looked for all the world like some of the little clay dolls Mary occasionally molded of brown clay for the village children, was not altogether surprising. Lollia was a pagan, you couldn't expect otherwise although she herself admitted she sometimes had her doubts, seeing how little good any of them had done the child.

To behold in Phyllis those same heathenish beliefs, however, was disquieting. Mary felt embarrassed, almost ashamed for Phyllis. If an uneasy thought crossed Mary's mind that to make the sign of the horns might also be a heathenish practice, she ignored it. Because no matter what her father and Mark said, how could you know positively that there wasn't such a thing as the evil eye? Besides, she always felt a little uncomfortable in her conscience when she made the sign, which proved that she didn't really believe in it. Or at least she didn't believe in it as much as lots of other people did.

The sun was sliding down the west as they hastened villageward, fearful lest the caravansary gate be locked at sunset. Cato was standing guard outside and he waved them kindly on when they asked if there was time to visit the village to buy honey bread. Oxen were being led down to the water, a string of donkeys passed, almost buried under swaying loads of grass, and at the entrance to the village a man was holding a sheep and a goat under either arm while a woman milked.

Phyllis bought a bowl of sheep's milk and shared it with

Mary. They would find no crumb of honey bread in all the town, the woman told them, nor would there be any honey for the baking until the new combs were lifted from the hives. The last of it had been sold to two merchant men who had come a fortnight ago to carry it to the city of Tiberias where King Herod was preparing a great banquet.

Within the caravansary there was such a cheerful noisiness of neighing donkeys and whuffling, plaintive-voiced camels, men talking and shouting, iron spoons scraping in bubbling brazen cauldrons, that Mary was not sorry they had not delayed to view the town. It must be spices and balms in the wrapped bales piled in the center, she thought, catching a whiff of some unfamiliar fragrance, or maybe it was sandal-wood or frankincense.

But it was the supper odors she sniffed most pleasurably, the fish the dark-skinned, turbaned foreigners were broiling over low charcoal braziers, the pancake loaves of barley bread Haephestium's bakers were taking hot from the stone ovens, the thickly bubbling stews of garlic-seasoned lentil and barley, the chunks of mutton and slices of onion sizzling on long skewers over the coals of Haephestium's fires. The Egyptian boys who held the skewers were shiny-faced with the heat as if their faces had been rubbed with oil, and Haephestium, bustling officiously from cauldron to caul-dron, wiped the perspiration from his brow with first one hand then the other.

Phyllis complained that the smell of sweaty beasts almost at her elbow took her appetite, but Mary noticed when the time came to fill their wooden chargers that Phyllis broke her bread to dip into the stew as hungrily as anybody.

As twilight drew on, the two sat with old Lollia and Rufus just inside the door of their earthen-floored cubicle where they could look out into the courtyard to see what was going on. Soon the serving women came to sit behind them, their task finished of helping cleanse the special chargers and cups reserved for the lord Sextus and his officers. At the rear of the tiny room, two of the women huddled over a little oil lamp to sew patches and mend tunics for Sextus' men.

Phyllis spread one end of her blue mantle over Rufus, who snuggled half asleep in Mary's lap, his good foot curled beneath his warm little body, the lame foot sticking out straight and stiff. "In case the foreigners have brought with them any of the demons that attack children," Phyllis explained in a whisper. And though Mary gave little credence to Phyllis' demons, she could but forgive her her paganism, seeing her affectionate concern for the child.

"There's that root of rue I've somewhere in my belongings," Lollia remembered, "but I'm saving it till we get home. The trouble is"—she flapped a leafy switch of ilex to drive away the flies—"the only trouble is I don't know which slave it might be has put the evil spell upon the child to lame him."

One of the serving women related, in a voice between a ravenish croak and a breathy whisper, a sight she had beheld not more than an hour since—beheld with her own eyes, if anyone should doubt. She was coming up from the pool with the little master's clothes which she and Fulvia had been washing, when they met three women carrying goatskin bags of flour balanced upon their heads. There was nothing strange about that, or wouldn't have been, except that one of them had a withered hand—a bad omen.

And surely enough, what was the first thing she beheld as she entered the caravansary enclosure—beheld with her own eyes, mind you!—but a black-bearded man in a dark jacket and striped turban stirring a cauldron. The cauldron steamed and bubbled, she could smell the smoke and grease, yet there was no fire under it—it was licked invisibly by magic flames.

"Enough, enough—you'll wake the child with your long-spun tales and mystifications." Lollia enjoyed no long-winded stories except those she herself could tell. "I hope you and Fulvia didn't leave the young master's best tunic hanging on a bush, like the last time."

Shadows were taking the great courtyard, it was growing dark. Here and there a smoky torch flared, lighting a group of gaming soldiers whose shadows leaped and danced like figures of grotesque genii as they shook the cup to toss the dice. A dog barked, a donkey brayed in its sleep, and at the far end of the courtyard a man called out in a strange tongue to still the dog.

One by one the serving women rolled themselves in their blankets and lay to sleep on the hard earthen floor, and after them Phyllis, and then old Lollia and Mary, with the sleeping child bedded soft on goose-feather pillows between them. Slowly the yellow moon swung up over the stone- and mud-brick wall. Silence took over the encampment.

Watching the moon climb the sky opposite the open door of the cubicle, Mary thought how at this very hour it would be shining down upon her own village. She thought of her father and of baby Saul, just learning to toddle half way across the room from his mother's knee to Simon's out- stretched, steadying hand. But it was Mark she thought longest of, Mark's face she pictured most clearly there in the quiet of the moonlight.

In a week or so she would be coming into the city of Tyre in the land of Phoenicia, the city by the sea toward which Mark had months ago turned his footsteps to enter into the service of the newly born king. . . . Somehow Mark would have heard of her coming, somehow he would find her where she was lodged. And having found her, he would never let her go. For what was it the prophet had said in the scroll the rabbi had given them to read, there in the hill pasture while Mark tended the flock—"For with God nothing shall be impossible."

VIII

LUCIUS

"STAND still now, master Rufus, be a good boy and let Lollia finish washing your face," the old nurse pleaded as the child ducked his little blond head to jerk free of her grip. The lap of her dress was wet and her sandals spotted where he had spattered the water from the brazen bowl.

"Just let me rub that streak of honey off your cheek." She made a futile dab with the wet washcloth. "Else when your big brother Cordus rides out from Tyre in his chariot to meet us he'll say, 'Whose dirty little boy is that?' If your face looks nice and clean I shouldn't be surprised if Cordus lets you ride in the chariot with him."

"Chay'ut!" the child screeched at the top of his voice, dodging and frisking like a playful puppy. "Wide chay'ut!"

"Not if you don't quiet down and behave yourself," Lollia warned sternly. Perhaps it was a mistake anyhow to get the child's hopes up about the chariot. Cordus was not the kind of person you could depend upon, and he seldom took more than passing notice of his little brother, though on this occasion he might show himself more affectionate, since it was all of a seven-month that he had not seen the little lad.

"You remember Cordus, don't you, little master—big

brother Cordus who lives in the house with you and your mother in Pompeii?" she reminded him anxiously, because his father would not like it if she had allowed the child to forget his home. "The big house with the stairsteps that go up and down—remember? and the fountain that splashes? and the runnels in the garden where you like to dabble and play you're a fish?"

"What's he like?" Mary questioned, handing Lollia a comb to complete the young master's toilet. "Cordus, I mean." At Lollia's bidding she was changing into her Sabbath dress before the men came for the saddlebags. "How does Cordus know his father will be arriving this afternoon?"

"Sextus sent a messenger on ahead from the last village where we stopped." With the complacent air of one who was kept fully informed of her lord's plans and purposes, Lollia relayed the news she had gathered only a short quarter-hour ago from Sextus' valet when she went to fetch Rufus from his father's tent.

"It was all arranged before we left Pompeii that Cordus should travel to Tyre, come springtime. Sextus wants him to have experience with treasuries and publicans so the emperor can sometime appoint him to serve at a post in the provinces.

"There now, master Rufus, see what Lollia's got for you to play with!" From under the folds of her skirts she drew a toy horse. It was carved of dark wood with a string to pull it, and the tail was of black horse-hair.

"Keep an eye on him, Mary, that he doesn't get himself dirty. He's to ride with his father this morning." Lollia tossed her wet dress at Mary to be packed while she draped herself in her best—a sulphurous yellow with borders of orange. "Help me pin the ends of my fillet under my knot before the men come to take down the tent.

"And I've a length of the same yellow to bind your hair." The ribbon was crumpled and the color quarreled with the scarlet wool of Mary's sash and the darker red of the borders of her dun-colored dress, but it was of silk and Mary was pleased to add so citified a touch to her costume.

Now that they had left the caravan route and were following the stone-paved road which the Romans had built eastward from the sea, they could easily ride two abreast. On this last stretch of the way Phyllis was riding at her husband's side, while Mary and Lollia kept each other company farther back in the train.

The road was busy with traffic to and from the city—every mile or two a train of pack-asses with bags of Egyptian grain and bales of Tyrian-dyed cloth destined for Damascus and Jerusalem, strings of slow-footed cattle being led down from the hill country with cumbersome sacks of charcoal, chariots, single or in squadrons, with Roman officials bound upon military or civil embassy for Caesar Augustus and private citizens on business of their own, horseback riders, couriers, pilgrims and country men on foot, and an occasional deliberate-gaited, solitary camel with a tied bag swagging heavily on either side of its hump.

"If there's a cockfight on," Lollia made shrewd comment as a troop of gay young gentlemen went trotting past upon sleek Arabian mounts, the one in the lead balancing before him in the saddle a cage of willow withe and plaited reed with a black-feathered cock, "mark my words, Mary, if it's a cockfight afoot, the lord Sextus will not lay eyes upon his elder son this day.

"No, that he won't," she prophesied darkly. "For wherever there's gaming with cocks, there you must look to find his lordship Cordus. And after, roistering and dicing with the other young aristocrats till all hours"—Mary could not be certain whether Lollia was deploring Cordus' idle habits or boasting of the company he kept—"and himself the most spendthrift of the lot."

It was a matter of continual surprise to Mary that there should be so much coming and going upon the road. Hardly a quarter hour went by without something different to see— an ox-sled with logs of cedar, a rotund old gentleman astride an ass, his short legs dangling, his crimson-striped robe flapping in the breeze, three or four donkeys creeping along under wrapped bales of some sweet-smelling stuff, a couple of slaves in leather breeches, the mules they were leading so extraordinarily valuable that each wore about its neck a string of blue glass beads as protection against some covetous evil eye.

When early in the afternoon Mary glimpsed in the distance between land and sky a strip of shimmering azure which Lollia declared was the ocean sea, it was hardly to be believed. "But I can see across it," she objected, not so much doubting Lollia's word as amazed and puzzled. "It's no wider than a river."

"You'll think different on shipboard with waves washing all round and never a speck of land in sight," was Lollia's somewhat gloomy prediction. She was no sailor; she did not take kindly to the roll and pitch of a masted trireme in flight before a freshening wind.

An hour later they came to a halt outside the city where the tax gatherers were stationed to take tally of whatever merchandise went in or out the city. "The tax is a tenth on oil," Mary heard one inform a lame man who came leading a donkey with a goatskin of oil on its back. She felt sorry for the man, his clothes were so ragged and he fished so worriedly through his old wallet to find the necessary coins.

It was his oil, pressed from olives grown on his own trees, she thought indignantly; what right had the Romans to wring money out of people who couldn't afford to pay?

Measures of grain, heads of cattle, skins of wine, bags of charcoal to be burned in city ovens, even the baskets of lettuce and radishes two women were carrying balanced on their heads the tax gatherers took strict toll of, scribbling the tallies down in their books. But because Sextus was a royal quaestor with sealed leather bags of tribute money for the treasury of Caesar Augustus, the tax men required no payment from him or his train.

It was not fair—Mary's cheeks reddened with resentment to think how unjust it was—that the tax gatherers should let a rich man pass just because he was a Roman. Anybody could see that the man with the wineskins hadn't enough to eat, nor the two women either—they were scrawny as winter reeds—yet they had to pay. Of course it was not Sextus' fault; it was the publicans who were to blame. They did not have things all their own way, however. Mary laughed to herself to see a canny old farmer, his face brown and creased as a walnut, reduce the taxable portion of his load of hay by feeding his donkey a thick bunch before he reached the toll booth.

One by one Titus the steward paid off the various provincials who had hired themselves into Sextus' service for the journey—the Egyptian boys and Haephestium's helper cooks, the dark-bearded men from Palestine whose pack-asses had borne the provisions and gear, the roustabouts who had set up the tents and foraged for fuel, and the two tall bearded stalwarts who had carried the litter for small Rufus to ride in, what time he was not sharing a donkey with Mary or Lollia or enjoying the eminence of his father's saddle.

What remained of supplies Titus divided among the men, apportioning to each a measure of flour, and to some, wedges of cheese and to others strings of dried figs. Their wooden chargers too they were allowed to keep, but the great bronze cauldrons and iron spoons and cups Haephestium would store in the soldiers' barracks within the city for succeeding journeys. It made Mary feel rather better about the

Roman taxes, seeing how freely Sextus gave of his possessions.

While Lollia and the other women waited in the shade of a dusty oleander clump for Sextus to finish his questioning of an obsequious tax collector and Titus his doling out of silver and copper coins to the donkey men, Mary rode Rufus pickaback in and out among the oleander bushes. She was a camel, she told him—and she made a most convincing hollow tinkling sound in her throat like a camel bell to prove it—and if he didn't stop snatching at the pink blossoms and hold on tight she would go galloping straight off to the desert without him. At which he squealed so shrilly in her ear and hugged her neck so tight she was forced to set him down upon a rock until she could get her breath again.

"And who are you, may I ask—that is, if you'll not think me impertinent for wanting to know?"

Mary raised her head to find herself confronting a stranger, taller than she, his hair the color of ripe wheat in the sun. "Or shouldn't I have asked?" His eyes, gray-blue, met hers with cheerful impudence.

Startled by the appearance of a young man where a moment ago there had been but sand and rocks and oleander shrubs, Mary gasped and stared. Her face was hot, she was still panting from the game she had been playing with the child, the yellow ribbon had come loose and a lock of hair had fallen over one eye. Intensely blue, the other eye looked out at him from under the dark lashes and the shadow of her wind-blown hair. For a moment she stood motionless, head uplifted, attentive as a fawn surprised by a hunter, in that breathless, fleeting interval before curiosity gives way to prudent fear.

The youth wore a tunic of fine white cloth, she saw—although it was not until later that she was aware of having noticed—and the short-sword at his belt was sheathed in brown-dyed leather.

"Perhaps you are Daphne?" he questioned humorously. "But no, for these shrubs are not laurels.

"Diana, of course, light of foot and swift as arrows in flight! It is to Diana then that I must bend the knee in homage."

Who Daphne was, or what connection there might be between Daphne and laurel trees, Mary had no notion, but Diana, she knew, was one of those false goddesses to whom the Romans bowed themselves down in heathen worship. . . . He was laughing at her, making fun of her appearance. Mary's cheeks burned hotter at the thought, her embarrassment doubled by her own awareness that the ribbon fillet was flopping about her ear and her hair was blown every whichway until it must look as disheveled as Lollia's straggling gray locks after a day on the road.

Well, if he thought that being a Roman gave him the right to make mock of her, he was mistaken, Mary told herself, summoning her temper to overcome her self-consciousness. She was every whit as good as he was, and maybe better, because she wasn't a pagan. If he supposed just because she was from the country that she didn't know more than to take up with city strangers, he would soon learn otherwise. So, with what she fancied was an expression of chill disdain—though the effect was somewhat weakened by a sticky smudge upon her chin where Rufus had pressed some crumbs of honey bread—Mary turned deliberately upon her heel, remembering barely in time to seize Rufus by the hand before she made for the security of Lollia's company.

She had gone scarcely a dozen steps when it occurred to her that the young man could be none other than Cordus. She had refused to make answer to a civil question Sextus' own son had put to her! If only Rufus had recognized him —but you couldn't expect a young child to remember so long. Maybe she could get Lollia to explain for her and smooth things over—

"Cordus?" the old nurse snorted. "The only place you're likely to behold the young lord Cordus is in Italy. About the time he was supposed to set sail he suffered some kind of ailment and his mother would not (or so he sent word by Flavius) by any argument be persuaded to let him risk his health in foreign lands." To judge from the way Lollia pursed her lips and looked down her nose, one might almost have got the impression that she was belittling the young man's malady.

"That was Lucius spoke to you. They sent him instead to help the lord Sextus and Titus. And as for acting civil

to Lucius, it's no great matter one way or t'other. He's no
but a freedman's son."

Relieved not to have given a member of Sextus' family
cause to think ill of her manners, Mary was still not altogether comfortable in her mind. Maybe she should have
spoken to Lucius. Perhaps he hadn't intended to make fun
of her; he might only have been wishing to tease. As she
smoothed her hair with Lollia's wooden comb and anchored
the yellow ribbon with one of the long bronze hairpins
which Phyllis had given her, it was some slight satisfaction
to remember that she was wearing her scarlet sash. Phyllis,
who had an eye for such things, said the color was becoming. And she didn't think Phyllis had said it just to flatter
her.

Titus had dismissed the last of the donkey men, Sextus
concluded his business with the servile publican, and now
the legionaries went marching off to the garrison the Romans maintained within the city, stepping briskly in single
file to the sound of a trumpet.

The half dozen soldiers who would guard the money bags
until they were safe under lock and key within the emper-
or's treasury took up their position on either side of the two
heavily burdened asses, the various officials mounted their
horses, Lollia and the serving women clambered with what
speed they could aboard their drooping donkeys, and Mary
managed with one arm to hold the small, tired Rufus upright before her on the saddle while she prodded her reluctant steed into action.

And thus, with the quaestor Sextus in the lead, the gold of his bracelets and necklet shining in the sun and the sharp-pointed spears of the legionaries fencing with iron the gold sealed from sight within the brown leather bags, Mary followed with the serving men and women into the city of Tyre.

IX

AT HEROD'S COMMAND

AT FIRST Mary thought that if she could have a few hours to herself, to walk up and down the streets of the city, she would somewhere come upon Mark. Or at least she would meet someone who would take him word that she was here in Tyre. For there must be others besides Mark who had made their way to the land of Phoenicia where Herod could not hinder them from entering the service of the infant king.

She and Lollia and Rufus were lodged together in a small room at the inn, with the two serving women who would accompany them to Italy occupying the alcoved recess at the rear. Until such time as a ship should be ready to sail, the others of Sextus' company—or so it seemed to Mary—were free to come and go as they pleased, while she must keep company with Lollia in the small courtyard around which the inn was built, tossing a leather ball for Rufus to catch or playing hide-and-find among the laurel shrubs or boosting him up to perch triumphantly upon a sagging limb of the pomegranate tree which scattered its crimson petals upon the black and white mosaic of the pavement. Only twice had Mary stepped beyond the door of the inn, and then no further than the baker's stall across the narrow street, to buy sweets for Lollia. Lollia was fond of sweets.

This afternoon, however, as soon after the midday siesta as shops were re-opened for business, Phyllis requested Mary's company. She had purchases to make and her husband would not permit her to go unattended.

"But you must wear my scarlet fillet—not that jaundiced yellow thing," she insisted. "There, that's better"—tilting her carefully curled dark head in critical appraisal—"to match your sash. Though of course blue is your color." Phyllis was expert, not to say artful, in the refinements of adornment. "Nobody'd ever call you a beauty, Mary, but your eyes do quite well."

Had it been some arcane secret known only to sorcerers which Phyllis was imparting, how to turn water into sweet white wine or a copper penny into a silver denarius, Mary could hardly have been more impressed by the information. Blue—her color was blue. She drew a long, eager breath and with the air breathed in a flattering conviction that she was now initiate of such mysteries of the feminine toilet as even the beauteous Queen of Sheba might have been glad to possess. The first thing when she got home she must tell Miriam about suiting colors to each other, because Miriam always liked to look pretty.

"To the market place," Phyllis gave command to the Egyptian slaves who waited at the door of the inn with the chairs Titus had ordered, "the shops where they sell dyed stuffs."

Even if it had been prophesied, she would not have believed it, Mary thought in a kind of daze of wonderment
whether this could actually be herself—wide awake too, not
dreaming or imagining. No, never in the world would she
have believed that she would ride in a chair like the high-
born ladies in Jerusalem whom Miriam told about. Yet here
she was, borne shoulder high along the thoroughfare.

Not even in Jerusalem could there be such a maze of
streets, closely walled with houses of plastered brick and
stone, many with an upper story and not a few with pil-
lared balconies. It was astounding. Wherever you turned
your eyes there was something new and different to see—a
fountain in the shape of a fish with water trickling from its
mouth, a silken banner hanging from an upper window, a
dignified old gentleman in a purple-bordered toga issuing
from a doorway with a courtly cat perched upon his
shoulder.

The nearer they came to the market place, the livelier the
streets grew. And in the square itself was such a kaleido-
scope of bright colors and pleasant din of sounds Mary
could have lingered there till set of sun, it was all so wonderfully strange and exciting. Shopkeepers tinkled little
bronze camel bells or tapped invitingly upon hollow wooden
chargers to invite customers, bare-legged fishermen hawked
their rainbow-scaled catch, still dripping with sea water,
kitchen slaves from households of the rich haggled with
sunbrowned country men over the price of radishes and
trussed geese. Except on the nearer side where the portico

of a Roman temple lifted its marble columns against the blue of the sky, the square was fronted with stalls and low-built shops, with a colonnade to make cool shade against the sun.

After the first glimpse it was toward the temple that Mary gazed longest, though not at the soaring shafts of fluted marble with their leaf-carved capitals, nor the ragged sellers of doves congregating about the base of the columns, nor yet at the bearded money changers who had set up their tables within the very temple entrance.

Along the portico, at the head of the broad flight of steps leading up from the stone-paved square, there extended a row of eight or ten writing tables where scribes scribbled pothooks for merchant men's tally or, lacking customers, took their ease on their folding stools. Swiftly Mary's eyes traveled along the row of tables, her breath coming short with the suddenness of the hope that throbbed in her throat.

But what she sought she did not find. And though a second time her eyes told over the writing men, figure by seated figure, importunate, as if by very strength of will she could conjure her hope into a living, breathing reality, the faces she saw remained those of strangers.

Reluctantly she followed Phyllis into a shop. Try as she would, she could not summon her attention to consider the lengths of cloth which the shopkeeper draped across the wooden counter for Phyllis to choose from. Some part of her mind kept tugging at her to turn her head to keep watch through the open shutter. For what if while she was helping Phyllis mull over the colors—fine-woven linens and soft Egyptian cottons, crimson and purple of the true royal, rose-color, magenta, peach-blossom pink, and each and all, so the smooth-tongued shopkeeper avowed, Tyrian-dyed and fadeless—what if at that very moment Mark should be passing by and she not see him!

Later, at the toy stall selecting something for Rufus—a yellow-painted clay whistle in the likeness of a duckling, since the charge for wooden toys was more than the penny Lollia had given her—Mary could still bolster her dwindling hope with the promise that she would persuade Lollia to let her come again on the morrow to the market square, alone and on foot. A chair was no way to go looking for someone in a crowd, it went too fast and you couldn't stop to speak with people to ask the kind of questions you needed to ask if you expected to get trace of someone you were looking for.

"You're not betrothed, I trust?" Lollia inquired suspiciously. "It isn't some plan you've been making to be wedded and keep on here in Tyre?"

Mary reddened. They were not betrothed, she said, Mark would rather serve the new king than take a wife.

"Then why waste your time?" Lollia was not unsympathetic, but young people lack judgment. And in spite of Mary's denial, it still might be that she had something up her sleeve. If she should take a notion to seek a change of employment, Lollia would be hard put to it to find another so capable and willing. The child liked her too, she had a way with children, she kept him happy and happiness is good for children.

"If the fellow had a mind to see you, he'd come looking for you."

Mark was not expecting her, Mary explained, feeling the red color mount to her forehead and wishing it wouldn't. She had nothing to be ashamed of, she told herself, it was only out of friendliness that she desired to see Mark.

"We've known each other since childhood." She tried to make it sound a commonplace. "We come from the same village."

Even if Lollia didn't approve, Mary tried to argue herself into thinking, she would not be deterred from doing what she wanted to do. Somebody was celebrating with a banquet at the inn, and sounds of men's voices, snatches of song and laughter, the piping of a flute and cymbals' lively tinkling floated up from the court, but it was not that which was keeping her from sleep, nor Lollia's purring snore at her ear, nor the muffled grunt and drone of the two serving women asleep in the alcove. Her own mind made her restless, thoughts crowding and jostling each other as though they had a life of their own.

Maybe Mark would approve no more than Lollia of her going about alone in a strange city, maybe she ought to take Claudia with her. But Claudia couldn't—she was busy all day long, and Fulvia too, mending and laundering in preparation for the sea voyage. There could be no harm in going to the market place; she would wear her old dress and nobody would pay any attention to her. . . . What if the search for Mark should lead all the way to the weaving sheds and dye-works? She might get lost, it was a bad neighborhood, there were thieves and runaway slaves, re-

spectable people wouldn't live there, Lollia said, on account
of the stench from the rotting shellfish the dye was made
of. Even here in the inn you could smell it when the breeze
blew from the landward side as it was blowing now. Mary
burrowed her nose under her elbow to hide from the odor.

She attempted to push to the bottom of her mind where
she could ignore it an unacknowledged fear that what Lollia had hinted at might be true, that for her to go seeking
Mark would cheapen her reputation and so make him think
the less of her. The misgiving would not down, it colored
all her thoughts. Things to which she had been able to shut
her eyes during the afternoon now returned to discomfort
her—laborers standing idle in the market place because no
man had hired them, a blind man with a ragged child to
lead him, a woman skeleton thin, begging a crust of bread.

"It isn't my penny," Mary had wanted to explain to her,
to clear herself of the accusation she read in the woman's
sad eyes. "I'd give it to you if I could." . . . Maybe she
should have given her the money anyhow. Rufus didn't need
the whistle, and as soon as she got any money she could
have paid Lollia back.

Maybe it was not too late to make it up to the woman.
She would save all her breakfast bread to take her when
she went to the market place to look for Mark. And when
she told Lollia, perhaps Lollia would give some of her
bread too.

But the morrow brought with it new duties. The goat
man had halted his flock as usual before the entrance to the

inn, with a long, quavering cry very like a lament, "Milk—fresh, fresh from the pasture—bring your bowls—fre-fre-fresh," the syllables rising and falling with a mournful music upon the misty morning air. While his two ragged, sunburned sons dashed back and forth waving their arms like flails and shouting to head off the several obstinate beasts bent upon escaping from the flock to explore a side street, Mary lent a steadying hand to the bronze cup Rufus was holding up to be filled.

The milk was still spurting into the cup, a thin, foamy stream, when Lucius came hurrying around the corner, the folds of his white wool toga flapping against his tanned legs with the haste of his stride. "The auspices are favorable," he announced with a grin, like an old friend, as though taking credit to himself for news he knew Mary would be glad to hear.

She stared at him blankly, not knowing what he was talking about, though it was impossible not to feel well disposed toward him, he was so blond and handsome and his grin was so disarming.

"The ship finished lading yesterday late, and I've been to the temple to make sacrifice for Sextus. The omens are for favoring winds and a safe voyage. We sail at the sixth hour, with the tide.

"How now, young man?" He tweaked Rufus playfully by the ear. "So greedy for a sip of milk you can't give me greeting?" And again to Mary, calling over his shoulder as he entered the inn, "Bid Lollia and the serving women have their gear ready. We board ship soon."

The sixth hour—noon—and already the second hour was well advanced! She could not—she would not go, was Mary's first swift thought; until she had seen Mark and talked with him and knew there was no coolness toward her on his part, she would not set foot aboard ship. They could sail without her.

On her way through the courtyard, however, and up the steep flight of steps to their room, a slow progress because of the shortness of Rufus' legs and his lameness, common-sense got the upper hand of emotion. In the end it was rea-son which had the last word. Lollia was depending upon her, she had promised to go to Pompeii, and she must keep her word.

"Lucius says to tell you we sail at the sixth hour," she in-formed the old nurse and the two women threading their needles to sew a border of red on a tunic for Rufus. "He says to make ready at once." If she sounded less than cheer-ful, nobody noticed.

Whether it was because there was no time for thought with all that must be done, folding Rufus' garments to pack neatly into a small leather trunk, wrapping his shoes and sandals in an old shirt to keep them from soiling the fresh tunics, fetching loaves of honey bread and a wicker basket of little sweet cakes, greasy and good, from the bake shop for Lollia's and the child's refreshment when the ship's ra-tions should lack flavor, and making a neat bundle of the toys and her own few belongings, Mary was beginning to share in the older women's bustling excitement.

And by the time they had boarded the masted trireme and Lucius had lingered in Mary's company to find a place on the quarterdeck where she and Rufus could safely stand to view the busy wharfs, a kind of adventurous elation, reckless rather than glad, made Mary half forget the heaviness that still cumbered some part of her mind.

"Is it your first voyage?" Lucius inquired, and without waiting for a reply, "Here, toss this into the water—now, before the oars stir—in token to Poseidon." He slipped into her hand a small, earth-colored clay dolphin. "And one for Rufus too. Now, both of you!"

Mary's dolphin struck the water first, then Lucius' and the child's in quick succession. A moment later the oars in triple tier broke the blue of the water into sliding, swirling silver. Beneath her feet Mary felt the deck gently sway and lift, there was a creaking sound of cordage and timbers. Rufus dragged at her hand, hopping up and down and yelping with excitement. The ship was moving.

"If you're a good boy," Lucius promised, "I'll show you over the ship as soon as I see whether your father has work for me to do.

"Another few minutes and we'll be under sail." He pointed for Rufus to look up at the great square of canvas criss-crossed with strips of leather for extra strength, but Mary thought it was to her he was really speaking. She was relieved that he was not holding it against her that at their first encounter she had acted unfriendly.

"You won't find it so easy to avoid my company on shipboard, Mary." His eyes sought hers in level, humorous gaze.

She pretended to be looking past him, at a sailor pulling on a rope. A dimple showed in her cheek, the wind burnished her hair to bronze.

Because of Rufus, Lollia and Mary were cabined on the quarterdeck between the huge, towering mainmast and the stern of the trireme, in one of the several cubicles designed for the use of the captain and privileged passengers. Amidships the deck was built lower, to accommodate the galley slaves seated at their oars on each side the ship, three tiers of them, one above the other—some hundred and seventy in number, Lucius said there were. Forward, in the forecastle, where the deck rose again, the crew had their place and the kegs of drinking water were ranged in balance, lashed to the rail, on either side of the auxiliary mast with its foresail, square-rigged like the great mainsail.

Below decks were makeshift bunks for passengers, together with the ship's stores and luggage, with the main cargo and the ship's ballast of heavy squared stones stowed underneath the middle deck. Although the ship carried a number of passengers besides those in Sextus' party, chiefly Roman merchants and civil and military agents of Augustus, with a few well-to-do Egyptian and Hebrew traders, it was primarily a wheatsailer, the *Triton,* a merchantman carrying wheat and cotton from Egypt to Italy.

At Tyre it had taken on Tyrian purple and bales of goat's hair, together with costly goods brought down by caravan from Persia and the Parthians, Lucius believed—beeswax, ivory and rhinoceros horn, frankincense, tortoise shell, rock crystal and quicksilver—as well as silk and amber from some region far to the northward where the Roman army had never penetrated. China, some called the name of the region, and others the Flowery Kingdom. . . . Mary thought of the black-bearded, turbaned strangers with knives at their belts, squatting beside their charcoal braziers in the dusk at the caravansary to cook their supper, and wondered whether the man with the bird that spoke words might have come from that distant land of flowers.

Already a trifle queasy with the ship's motion as the oars came to rest and the sails took over with the freshening breeze, Lollia could not be coaxed to have a look at the galley. "I can stand right here and tell it's no appetizing dish the cook will be serving up, come mealtime," she declared gloomily.

"If you're minded to smell it closer, Mary, all I ask is you keep tight hold of the young master's hand so he doesn't fall overboard. Look to it, Lucius, you don't keep her long. I may have need of her."

The galley fires lay in two or three holes in the middle of a large block of clay and brick, with cooking pans just the right size to fit over the fire holes. The cook, clad only in a loin cloth, a mild little man with small, winking eyes, quickly recovered from his surprise at sight of a girl to proffer them a taste of the stew he was stirring, an oily mixture of barley, lentils, garlic, goat's meat, and dried fish. When Rufus choked upon a bone, Lucius promptly stuck a finger down his throat to dislodge it, which made Mary even more certain she was going to like the young man.

"Let the laddie eat his fill." The cook was complimented to have the child reach for the greasy ladle a second time. "When this mess is gone, there'll be no more goat. The wetter the waves, the drier the fish in the ship's galley!" He chuckled at his own witticism, but Lucius either had not heard or did not wish to humor him, and it was only Mary who smiled.

Back on the quarterdeck again, Lucius was in no haste to go below to assist Titus with the account books. If his talk at times tended somewhat toward the boastful, he was perhaps not entirely to blame. Mary's absorption in whatever he had to say, the wind ruffling her hair and flushing her face, her eyes alight to think how experienced in the ways of the world and intelligent above the ordinary and altogether charming and admirable this new friend she had made, no doubt may have prompted Lucius to enlarge upon his own accomplishments.

He was not regretful to be leaving Tyre, he said, it could scarcely interest one who had twice visited Rome. Nevertheless he had turned to profitable account the weeks he had been obliged to await the arrival of Sextus, and both his own purse and that of his father Lupinus would gain thereby.

Had it been Cordus now—Lucius lowered his voice and glanced to both sides to make sure nobody would overhear—Cordus would have wagered on every cock in the port and diced the nights away, piling up a mountain of debts for his father to pay. Lucius did not believe in gambling; it was a waste of good money.

At a fraction of their true value Lucius had been buying skins the Arabs brought down from the desert to barter in Tyre, doe skins soft as milk, and kid and camel skins. His father was a shoemaker and prosperous, his customers noblemen and senators and aristocratic ladies, willing to pay a fat price for fancy shoes and sandals.

Lucius was partner in his father Lupinus' shop, although as soon as he got a little more money together he intended to buy himself a commission in the imperial service. Nor could the lord Sextus very well refuse to stand as his patron, seeing that he had already been patron all these years to Lupinus. For it had been Lupinus' good fortune to be born into the house of Sextus' father, son of a Greek kitchen slave and one of the captives the great Julius Caesar had brought back as slaves from some campaign against the German barbarians.

As reward to Lupinus for saving Sextus' life during the course of a wild boar hunt—another stroke of good luck that it had happened to be Lupinus instead of another, else Lucius would have been born a slave instead of the son of a freedman—Sextus had not only given Lupinus his freedom but had set him up in business.

"There's money in shoes, Mary, I don't mind telling you. When I say that my father counts his daily profit not in pennies, mind you, but in sesterces and denarii, I'm not boasting. Enough to marry my sister off with a dowry worthy the daughter of a banker, and still not dent my father's cash box.

"But unless you're content to be numbered all your life among the plebeians"—which obviously Lucius was not—"you must have the honor of office as well as cash to offer as qualification. Of course I'll have to start at the bottom in some paltry office," he was frank to admit, "and even then it'll cost me a pretty sum—four or five thousand denarii at the very least.

"You don't think it's too dear to pay for the right to wear a finger ring of gold and a purple stripe on my tunic and sit in a privileged section at the theater?" He was smiling, as though to scoff at the pomp and trappings of the minor nobility. Mary was glad he did not set too great a value upon outward show. "Oh, yes, and on festal days to wear a mantle with purple stripes?

"The fact is," Lucius took Mary further into his confidence, "there's money in shoes but no future. The equestrian order has the wholesale trade and banking entirely in their hands, which is why it's absolutely necessary for me to get out of the plebeian class into that order. It won't be easy, you understand, but I'll manage somehow."

Had Lucius already passed the barriers into the society of the equites, the wealthy merchant nobility, he could hardly have spoken with greater self-assurance. But it was a cocksureness so agreeably tempered with friendliness and easy good humor that Mary was more than willing to accept him at his own evaluation.

"You don't think I'm overreaching myself to aim at service under the emperor?" he inquired with an air of mock humility, making a jest of it. "Some lowly post is all I ask, please remember."

If the world went according to merit, Mary thought, then Lucius would be welcomed with open arms into the order of the equites. (Though who or what the equestrian order was, she was not at all clear.) They ought to be glad to have him. But she did not say so, lest he might get the impression that she sought through flattery to win his friendship.

One of her friends, she told him, clutching Rufus more firmly with one hand and grabbing with the other at the ship's rail to steady herself as the vessel mounted a slow-rolling wave, a boy from her own village whom she had known all her life, was now in the service of a king.

"Under Herod, you mean? In Jerusalem?"

It was not Herod but a new king under whom Mark was serving, she explained. What his name might be she did not know, but he was yet in his infancy, no more than five or six months old.

Lucius looked grave. "I don't wish to be discouraging," he said, "and you've no cause to be uneasy on your friend's account, but if there's any truth to rumor I doubt whether anyone is serving the king you speak of."

It was common talk in Tyre, he went on to say, the stern measures Herod had taken to make certain that another would not usurp his throne. For three magi had come out of the East, so the rumor ran, to pay homage to a child born king of the Jews. Which, when Herod heard, had made him half mad with fear and rage against the child. And since it was not known—or if known, kept secret—who the young child was or where to be found, Herod had taken no chances but dispatched his soldiers widespread throughout Judea.

"They didn't—the soldiers didn't—" The word froze on Mary's tongue; she could not say it.

"All children of two years of age and under. Slain by the sword—it was Herod's command." Then, noting the white, pinched look of her face, as if she were suddenly ill and suffering, Lucius surmised there must be some particular child for whose life she feared. "You can be sure that the soldiers would never bother themselves about so insignificant a hamlet as you say yours is," he declared.

"If it were a village on a caravan trail or a road, or even in some remote valley, it would be different. But if I know soldiers"—the seriousness of his manner, the steadiness of his gaze as his eyes met hers would have convinced one even less desperately anxious to believe than Mary—"Herod's soldiers would find it convenient to overlook a handful of houses they'd have to climb a mountain to get at, knowing that by the time they got there, the young children would all have been spirited away."

"It is true, yes, what you say, Lucius, it would have happened so." The fear which had clutched at Mary's heart was relaxing, it was no longer an effort to draw breath. "Long before the soldiers got there, my father would have hidden baby Saul in a cave. There are lots of caves in our mountains.

"Or if Father was away, Miriam would," Mary reasoned aloud. "She knows where the cave is we sometimes fold the sheep in in stormy weather. If it was anything to do with the baby, she'd be brave.

"Miriam's the baby's mother," she explained. The color was coming back into her face and she looked more like herself. "I'm sure he's safe—Saul, I mean—but I wish I could be certain." Her eyes were still anxious.

"I think we can manage that," Lucius promised, his hand, warm and reassuring, taking hers for a moment within his where it rested upon the ship's rail. "The lord Sextus has deputies in Judea who can find out for you. Would you like me to put the request to him? Because he's always having to send them word by messengers."

She would never, she thought, be able to repay Lucius for his kindness. "I have no words to thank you— And would you," she interrupted herself to beseech a second favor, "would it be amiss to request Sextus' messenger to find out whether the other baby is safe? The one the magi came to see, I mean?" She could not rest content until she knew that all was well with the child Mark had beheld cradled in the hay of the manger—that other Mary's child for whom the star had shone in the heavens. Surely, oh, surely the baby's father would have known where to hide him safe from Herod's soldiers! If only there were some way of finding out! She would not let herself believe but that he was safe as her own little Saul.

Sextus would be glad to give orders to his deputies to find out about the other child as well, Lucius assured her. That's what deputies were for, to carry out their lord's commands.

X

THE SATURNALIA

THE LADY Livia was in an ill humor. Usually by this hour of afternoon her toilet was completed, her henna-colored hair curled and coifed, her cheeks and lips and eyebrows beautifully painted, and she would come forth from her bedroom to step daintily along the colonnade of the inner courtyard to where two serving women waited in the vestibule to escort her wherever she desired to go.

Sometimes, if she happened to be in a gracious mood, she might flutter a jeweled hand in gesture of goodbye as she passed her little son Rufus playing beside the tiled pool in the center of the peristyle, or even pause a moment—careful to draw her long skirts and the folds of her bright mantle aside lest the child touch them—to tell him he must be a good boy and do as Mary bade him. To judge, however, from the cringing haste with which a slave ran from the lady Livia's room to fill a basin at the fountain and the petulance of the voice that echoed briefly through the courtyard before the curtains closed again, this was not one of the lady's more amiable days.

Mary broke a twig from a leafless rose bush to set up as mast in the scrap of papyrus Rufus was sailing on the pool, and pinned back the sleeve of his short woolen cloak to keep it from the wet. She wished Lollia would hurry with the directions she was giving the sewing women so they could be gone about their errands before the lady Livia appeared.

The rumor whispered among the slaves of the household had it that the young lord Cordus had been robbed last evening. Gaius the cook had been gossiping about it with Ulpian the confectioner when Mary went to the kitchen at noon to get an apple tart for the little master's second breakfast. Since neither Gaius nor Ulpian was a slave and both could get high wages in any of a score of households whenever they were a mind to, because of the demand for chefs so superior as they to the common run, they had not troubled to change the topic of conversation nor lower their voices at Mary's entrance.

The theft had occurred at the baths. While Cordus was conversing with some other young gentlemen in the palestra —no, Ulpian interrupted, they were in the tepidarium, listening to a program of flute songs while the bath attendants gave them a rub-down—a sneak thief had crept into the dressing room and made off with Cordus' clothes.

Only his shoes had been taken, Ulpian corrected Gaius again, it was in one of his shoes that Cordus had hidden the ruby.

Cordus' toga had disappeared along with his shoes, Gaius insisted, and it was not a ruby the lady Livia had given him to sell to pay off this last lot of gambling debts, but a pearl of great price. If Ulpian wasn't willing to take Gaius' word for it, all he had to do was walk past the second-hand clothes dealer's shop in the corner of the forum and Gaius would wager a silver denarius Ulpian would see Cordus' very toga hanging in the doorway.

"Well, toga or no toga," Ulpian commented, tossing a sticky ball of honey-sweetened almond paste carelessly into the air to catch it like a juggler upon the tip of a knife, "his lady mother'll be spleeny when she gets wind of it. Hornets in the honey, tra la, wasps at the wine!" he caroled derisively, with a wink at Mary who pretended to believe it was not she but Gaius he was winking at.

It would not be Cordus his mother would be out of temper with, Mary knew. Cordus could wind the lady Livia around his little finger.

"Are you ready, Mary?" Lollia came padding from the kitchen end of the courtyard. "Don't keep me waiting, the afternoon's already half gone." Although Lollia was as anxious as Mary to flee the lady Livia's tongue while yet there was time, she preferred to make a convenient fiction of the need for haste before the shops should be closed.

The vintage season was at end and the calendar was entering December. The flowers were shriveled with frost that had made a mosaic of color about the tiled pool—roses and lilies, fuschias and love-in-idleness—and the smoldering magenta of bougainvillaea blossoms was long since faded that had blanketed the walls of the courtyard and spilled down the carved stone columns of the peristyle.

The neatly pruned lemon trees in the huge majolica vases at either end of the enclosure kept their color, but it was not the green of spring. Winter was already at the door. Already the fires had been lighted in the hollowed-out place under the floor in the center of the house, the heat was already traveling up through hollow tiles to warm the walls of the more important rooms, particularly the lady Livia's quarters, for she could not abide the cold.

Before the heavy rains should begin, however, and frosty mists darken and chill the sun, there was the mid-December Saturnalia to look forward to, and it was that which provided Lollia with an excuse to go shopping. She must purchase a piece of red cloth to make a pointed cap for the little master for the festival days.

"There'll be gay doings, come Saturn's thanksgiving," she reminded Mary, the pleasures of the celebration having been frequently on Lollia's tongue of late. Now that they had got through the atrium and vestibule and safely out into the street, she had quite perked up, like a plump old hen preening itself upon a clever escape from some imagined danger. "Such singing and laughing as you never heard, and merrymaking till you'd think it was the Golden Age like the good old days when Saturn reigned on earth.

"More's the pity he can't rule now, to make everybody rich and everybody equal." It was a pious wish, but empty, uttered to please the ears of the god who had been born son of Earth and Sky, should he happen at the moment to be listening.

Lollia had no desire to see the world changed, she was well satisfied with things as they were. Not only was she a plebeian and free, but as trusted nurse in the household of a wealthy patrician she could claim considerable prestige among those of her friends who were less well situated. And as for having the slaves all set free and equal to everyone else, as they were said to have been in Saturn's reign, what good could come of that? Slaves were base by nature; they were born to be slaves.

"Still, so long as Saturn's willing to see to the vines and wheat fields," she continued in a loud, cheerful voice for the god's benefit rather than Mary's information, "we've nothing to complain about." It cost nothing to speak a word of praise for the god of abundant harvests, and who knew but that in return he might show some unexpected favor?

"Saturn never lets us Romans lack for wine or victual, and this year he's filled every bin and storehouse to overflowing, and not a wine-press stands idle. It's little enough we can do to hold thanksgiving in his honor."

Already booths were being set up in the market place in anticipation of the coming Saturnalia, and at the shop where Lollia stopped to buy a miniature cart for Rufus with two clay wheels that turned on a wooden axle, a number of doll-makers were busied at turning out little terra-cotta images from earthenware molds. Every child in Pompeii would want a doll for the doll fair.

While Lollia bargained in the cloth bazaar, Mary remained outside in the forum with Rufus. A sturdy little boy and quick of movement although his lame foot sometimes tripped him and made him fall, he was always chasing something, the present object of his chase being the pigeons that flocked upon the steps of the temple where someone had spilled part of a votive offering intended for Jupiter's altar. Though the child never quite succeeded in laying hands upon any of the warily deliberate birds, it was a game of which he never tired.

Baby Saul would enjoy running after pigeons too, Mary thought, and by now he must be grown big enough to be almost as steady on his feet as Rufus. Only it would be chickens that he would be chasing, the old rooster squawking and the hens cackling as crazily as if it were a fox crept into the yard instead of a curly-headed two-year-old toddler. For more than a two-month ago one of the lord Sextus' agents had brought word that all was indeed well with the house of Simon. And Simon himself, in the letter the agent had fetched to Mary, said that Herod's soldiers had not come near the village with their swords and spears, but if they had, Simon would have known in what secret cave to hide his little son. And he hoped all was well with Mary as it was with Miriam and Saul.

Of the letter which had come folded within Simon's painstaking, briefly worded page Mary had spoken to no one. Most certainly not to Drusilla, Lucius' seventeen-year-old sister, although during this past seven-month she had become fast friend to Mary and Mary had told her much about Mark—how wise he was in the knowledge of books,

how quietly mannered and yet so strong there was none in
the village could best him at wrestling, and how he had
journeyed to the city of Tyre to enter the service of a newly
born king, though whether that new king were still alive

Mary could not truly say. They were not betrothed, she made it plain; Mark was poor, it might be years before he could afford a house and wife.

Drusilla, Mary knew, was far from persuaded that the feeling between her and Mark was no more than one of ordinary friendship between two persons who had grown up together in the same small village. And it may have been that Mary was not altogether unwilling to have Drusilla believe that an understanding existed between them, and that as soon as Mark possibly could, he would have his father make the necessary arrangements with Simon for the betrothal and marriage. For Drusilla maintained that any-one as talented as Mary said Mark was, was bound to come soon to the notice of important people who would put him in the way of advancing his fortunes.

"And then," she teased Mary, ducking out of reach before Mary could catch her by the shoulder to pommel her for such shameless impudence, "then we'll see whose wedding torch is lighted next "

"It's not true," Mary denied it, blushing. "You don't know what you are talking about!" Drusilla only laughed and would not be convinced.

Of late, however, Mary had ceased to mention Mark, and perhaps he was less often in her thoughts. Because Mark's letter, which Simon had enclosed within his own to her, was certainly not so personal that she must keep it secret. Quite the opposite—it might have been equally addressed to a trusted friend or a chance acquaintance.

He had found employment in Tyre, he wrote, at first in the dye-works and later with an elderly physician with whom he now purposed to remain. The name of the physician was Philip, he was a Greek, and the manner of Mark's entering his service had been thus: A chariot wheel had brushed against a young man on the road passing the dye-plant whom Mark, happening to be at hand, had helped to his feet. Seeing that one arm hung limp, Mark had bound it flat against a straight stick, using his own dye-stained tunic for bandage, having no other.

Some days later he had been summoned from the dye-pit to the overseer's office where a stranger inquired how he had learned to set a bone in splints. Tending his father's flock, Mark had explained. No mountain shepherd but must know to bind a broken leg of sheep and goat; the older shepherds teach the younger.

After some further conversation the man said he was physician to the injured youth and if Mark desired to apprentice himself Philip would be willing to employ him. To make a long story short, Mark wrote Mary, that was now his occupation. Because it had seemed to him then, as it seemed to him now, that there was no work he might do more serviceable to the new-born king than trying to bring health and healing to those of his people who were ill and in pain.

In conclusion Mark wished for Mary good health. He hoped she had thought better of her plan to go dwell among the pagan Romans and was still biding at home among her own people.

As Mary read, a band seemed to draw tight about her chest, the page blurred, and when she came to the place at the end where Mark's name was signed and still had found no word to which she could hold that nothing had changed between them, it was as though the gates had been closed to a walled city and she were shut outside.

"He couldn't put anything in writing," she attempted to convince herself. "He expected me to read between the lines."

The argument was weak. Even a third or fourth reading discovered no sentence which suggested more than it plainly stated. "He hasn't got over my defying him about Pompeii." That Mark intended to show by the impersonal tone of his letter that he was still vexed was less painful for Mary to believe than that he no longer regarded her as different from his other friends. "He thinks I ought to do exactly as he says.

"Let him stay in a huff if he wants to, it's nothing to me!" But it was her own anger she was fanning into flame to thaw the chill that spread along her heart. "I'll put him out of my mind, I'll never give him another thought."

Nevertheless it was of Mark that she was thinking now. The stone-paved market place had ceased to exist, the shops were vanished, the sanctuary of Apollo, the open colonnades where togaed Pompeians walked leisurely up and down, gossiping and chaffering. Rufus' headlong sallies back and forth across the portico of Jupiter's temple, the flutter of pigeons, even the massive bulk of the mountain Vesuvius dark in the background against the blue of the sky were as if they had never been.

It was Mark's face that Mary saw, his troubled frown, his eyes gentle with compassion, his hands skilled and firm as he knelt in his old brown shepherd's cloak beside the pallet of some ailing child. . . . If ever it should happen that little Saul should fall ill, Mark would know to make him well again.

"Are you deaf, Mary, that you can't hear?" It was Lollia, beckoning from the foot of the temple steps. "How many times must I call you?"

At sound of Lollia's voice the paved forum swung back into place again, the stately colonnade surrounding it on three sides, the shops with their shutters opened wide to the afternoon sun, the marble statues of famous men, the great basilica where lawyers argued their cases in the courts of law, the temple of Jupiter with the pink-toed pigeons fluttering just out of Rufus' reach.

Almost before the sewing women had finished stitching the seams of a new dress for Mary for the Saturnalia, the holidays were upon them. The house had been cleansed and garnished, upstairs and down, and garlands of evergreens and bright holly berries brought from the country to decorate the banquet hall and atrium and courtyard. From kitchen and bake-ovens there issued odors so tantalizing of roasting goose and haunch of venison, of fish in piquant sauce and oysters broiling on a grill with breasts of pheasants that involuntarily Mary slowed her step to breathe in the rich aroma whenever she crossed the courtyard. And a single whiff of the spicy fragrances wafted from Ulpian's oven, of honeyed pastries of quince and fig, of pears baking in cinnamon sauce and sweet cakes thick with nuts and brown with ginger gave proof that Ulpian was master of the confectioner's craft.

The lord Sextus had taken leave of his duties in Rome to spend the holidays with his family. It was not Mary's imagination, she was sure, that the household took on a calmer atmosphere when he was at home, the lady Livia's voice echoed less querulously through the courtyard, the slaves walked upright instead of scurrying with bent heads like harried animals, there was less bickering in kitchen and storerooms and less of furtive whispering behind posts and corners.

The young lord Cordus put in more frequent appearances too, and all but one of the half score willow cages of game cocks that to the exasperation of the gardeners usually cluttered the benches in the formal flower garden at the rear of the house, were vanished. "He pays a tidy sum to the gamekeeper that has the shop in the forum to keep the cocks while his father's in Pompeii." There was nothing went on but Lollia knew about it.

"He's sly, that Cordus, and his mother abets him in his extravagances. They don't either of 'em want the master to know what sums he squanders on gaming. And just as much at dicing too— It's a wonder his father's not bankrupt."

Nevertheless, although Lollia might sometimes frown upon that young gentleman's prodigal habits and sometimes moralize how times had changed since she was a girl— the young patricians used not waste their days in idleness and half the nights, and what was the emperor thinking of not to put a stop to such things—she was proud rather than otherwise of Cordus' lavish spending. It betokened the true aristocrat, one born to the purple, not having to work and worm his way upward as Lucius was ambitiously set upon doing.

"If it had pleased the gods to have you born a patrician with a gold spoon in your mouth," she sometimes remarked in Cordus' defense, "it would be folly to eat with your fingers."

Though it seemed to Mary wrong that Cordus should have money to throw away, while in the alleys of his own Pompeii there were plebeians who lived no better than slaves, they were so poor, she too judged him without severity. For when Cordus was in a jolly mood, his cock victorious or himself a winner at dice, it was a pleasure to see how kindly he took notice of little Rufus and how friendly his greeting if he happened to meet you in the courtyard or on the street. He was somewhat plumpish of figure, with a sharp nose like his mother's, his eyes small and close-set like hers and pale of color, but they lighted up when he smiled. Now that it was the holiday season, he had much to make him smile.

So too had Mary, for that matter. Lollia was assuming sole care of Rufus to let Mary enjoy the opening days of the festival with Drusilla. On the second day there would be an exchange of gifts, and Mary's were already wrapped ready for presentation, a round cinnamon honey cake from the baker's in the forum for Lollia, with eyes and mouth of sun-dried grapes so that you couldn't help laughing as you looked at it, it was so like a pudgy little face; a whistle for Rufus such as the youngest goat herds use, which Mary herself had been at pains to hollow out of a willow wand; and for Drusilla and her mother Paulina, two of the three mushroom-shaped marzipan confections Ulpian had given her.

"In case there's no crumb left from the master's banquet for us poor mice to nibble," he joked solemnly.

To look at Ulpian you might think he fared the year round on cabbage soup and gristle, he was so thin and lanky, but Mary never went into the kitchen or bake-room but he was munching at something—a knucklebone of roast pig, a goose-liver pâté, wing of pheasant or guinea fowl, or perhaps a cut of cold roast venison. For sweets he had no taste, he complained; he had surfeited of them in his youth.

Mary felt a little guilty not to share the marzipan mushrooms with Lollia, but she had already bought her the honey cake. Besides, although the worthy Lollia would have scorned to steal, she had ways of her own of appropriating to herself occasional tempting tidbits from the master's table.

Wedged in the crowd which thronged the market square, Mary stood on tiptoe to view the procession approaching the temple with votive offerings for the god in whose honor all Italy was holding thanksgiving. At one elbow was Drusilla, at the other Drusilla's gray-haired mother, with Lupinus a stout bulwark behind them to keep the crowd from pressing too close. The morning mists were lifting, the first rays of the December sun filtered iridescent through the haze. The air was chill and smelled of the sea; it would be a clear day.

"Here you are at last!"

It was Lucius, speaking as though it were they, not he, pushing through the crowd to arrive at the last minute. He carried his blond head so high, his toga was of such fine white wool, his manner so pleasantly important—not at all officious or arrogant—that those nearest were pleased to move aside to make room for him.

"I've just done old Sejanus a favor," he remarked in a lower tone. The words were for his father but his smile was for Mary. "Let's hope he remembers it when I ask a favor of him, the old skinflint."

A trumpet sounded, and then another and another in measured succession. Silence fell upon the crowd; through all the thronged forum was no voice heard save those of the bronze-throated horns proclaiming the arrival of the god.

Mary caught a glimpse of men marching impressively two by two, carrying fasces wreathed with olive leaves and sprays of wheat. Lictors, Lucius whispered they were, who attend upon high magistrates. Two sleek white oxen followed, their horns gilded and hung with garlands of holly and laurel, and then priests in solemn file, and last of all, trundling past on heavy wheels, a great image of the god Saturn, the stone face painted with vermilion because it was a festal day.

Lupinus would have given Mary a vial of oil and a handful of grain to make sacrifice to Saturn, but she said she could not, being no Roman. "Why not show a little kindness to the god?" Lucius whispered. "To please my mother if for no other reason."

Still Mary would not, though she did not ask herself whether it was because some thought crossed her mind what her father or Mark might think, or whether it was for some deeper reason.

If Lucius was disappointed, he did not show it. "We'll make a proper Roman of you yet," he threatened lightly. "You're already more a Pompeian than Judean, you can't deny it." His eyes, meeting hers, told her plainly that she had found favor in his sight. "Ask my mother here if she doesn't think so too."

"It's only the new cloak Lollia made me get for the holidays," Mary countered gaily. She hoped nobody noticed that she was blushing. "A country mouse tricked out like a city cousin."

Nevertheless she could not help being flattered to be likened to a Pompeian, the ladies were so fashionable and comely to look upon. Lucius was no more than making a friendly remark so she wouldn't feel herself an outsider, she told herself; he hadn't really meant it. She was glad now that Lollia had insisted upon the new costume, costly though it had seemed; she might have shamed Lucius and the others had she worn shabby apparel. And if she took care of the new garments so they lasted a long time, they would not be dear in the long run.

And indeed she intended to be extraordinarily careful of the three garments the lady Livia's sewing women had cut and seamed for her—a long tunic of white wool reaching to her ankles, a short-sleeved, girded stola that fitted over the tunic, falling in many folds to the ground, and an outer mantle for street wear, draped like a toga and drawn up over the back of her head when the weather was cold as it was today. Lollia had advised red-dyed cloth or magenta for the mantle, but Mary had held out for the blue color. It seemed vanity to think it—Mary blushed again with self-consciousness—but maybe it was because the blue color called attention to her eyes that Lucius had looked at her the way he had.

The merrymaking which began in mid-afternoon Mary watched with Drusilla and Paulina from the housetop, for the carnival parade led along the street where Lupinus had his shop and house. Every balcony within sight on the narrow street had its spectators, and the housetops too, mostly women and children, laughing to see a donkey with wings attached to his shoulders and the frolicsome pranks of the masked attendants who waited upon the fortunate fellow who had been chosen "King of Saturnalia."

Borne upon a litter, crowned with gilded laurel and bearing a scepter as though he were an emperor celebrating a triumph, his face painted with vermilion like Saturn's, the king of the holidays bowed regally right and left and lifted his garlanded scepter with a royal air to acknowledge the cheers that greeted him or to issue a command to one of his followers. Whatever command he might make, Drusilla told Mary, must be fulfilled, no matter how absurd or silly—to go on all fours like a donkey, to find a young pig and bring it to him swaddled like a new-born infant, or to leap into the air or walk backwards or whatever else his whim pleased him to command.

Last year's king had commanded two patricians to pull their own chariot and let the horses ride, but of course they couldn't get even one horse into the chariot, much less two, though masqueraders rushed by the dozens to lend a hand till you couldn't tell which were horses bucking and kicking out with their heels and which were men. When the horses broke loose and ran away and both wheels fell off the chariot, the king ordered the noblemen put in chains to follow after him like captives brought back from the wars, because they had not done as he told them. Drusilla had laughed till her ribs ached, it was so funny.

"*Io! Io! Io!*" The carnival crowd was shouting, the cymbals clashed, trumpets blared, flutes piped piercing shrill. "*Io! Io! Io!*"

A company of youths went cavorting by in trousers borrowed from the barbarian Gauls or Germans, and others decked out in women's clothes with fans and sunshades and upon their heads yellow-dyed wigs built up towerlike with curls and plaits in the latest style, so ridiculously resembling the lady Livia's most recent hair-do that it seemed to Mary the most comical sight she had ever seen. Wouldn't she give a new penny to behold that lady's expression when the be-wigged maskers pranced past her balcony!

"There's someone signaling you, Mary, see, the one in crimson stripes with the holly wreath," Drusilla giggled, pointing. "It's Lucius, I knew he'd have an eye out for you."

But later, when another of the masked figures in red pointed cap looked upward to wave at them on the roof, Drusilla turned her head away, frowning. "It's Sejanus," her mother reminded her. "Remember he sent word by your father to be watching for him, he'd be wearing purple."

Whether it was the unhappy expression upon Drusilla's face or the troubled look of her mother, it struck Mary that they had both suddenly lost their holiday mood. Between mother and daughter there was a marked resemblance, despite the difference in years which had dimmed and grayed the color of Paulina's hair and brought wrinkles to her brow.

It was from his mother that Lucius had his blond coloring—Paulina, like her husband, had been born of a German slave—and his pleasant manner. Lupinus was all hard work and ambition, with no time to spare for the little kindnesses and amenities which give to life an unobtrusive grace. He was a rich man and intended to be richer. If it lay within his power—and he was confident that it did—he would before he died see to it that his son and daughter were accepted in the society of the merchant nobles, although he himself, because of his lowly birth, could never hope to rise above the ranks of freedmen.

"The sky's blue as summer." Mary attempted to make conversation, to take Drusilla's mind off whatever it was that was damping her spirits. It was not like Drusilla to be moody. "And look how blue the sea is too."

Off to the right, beyond the wide expanse of rooftops that sloped under shadowy green of pines and dark of slender cypresses irregularly downward toward the bay, the water shone blue as the wild iris that in springtime channeled the valleys of Mary's own land.

"The wind blows cold." Drusilla shivered. "There's a cloud gathering landward over Vesuvius. Let's go within to warm our hands at the braziers."

"When dusk falls," Paulina promised Mary, "we'll mount to the roof again for you to see the street illuminated in Saturn's honor—candles set in the niches and lamps hanging from the doorways. We mustn't forget, Drusilla, to set our lamps alight."

Drusilla made no answer. Perhaps she had not heard.

As Mary followed the others down the narrow stairway into the courtyard, she remembered something she had all but forgotten—how in her own country the people would be lighting their lamps too, not for some graven image but in remembrance of the brave Maccabees who long, long ago had delivered them from persecution.

Above the sounds of carousal in the street, the wild shouts, the brazen trumpets echoing with a muted revelry through the walls of the courtyard, she heard in her thought the sonorous refrain—*Shammai Israel, Adonai eleënu, Adonai echod*—"Hear, O Israel: the Lord is our God, the Lord is one." . . . There was a knot in her throat.

Whatever it was Drusilla was saying to her about the feast on the morrow, she only half heard. For another memory had returned to haunt her mind with homesickness and longing—the memory of the light which Mark had seen— the star which had stood over Bethlehem, brighter and more beautiful than a thousand Roman candles. . . . And the child who had been cradled in the manger . . . where now did he lay his head?

XI

A WEDDING

Mary could not imagine what possessed Lollia of late to make her act so self-important. Not that Lollia had ever held herself in low esteem. "The pillar that props the palace," Ulpian dubbed her behind her back, but indulgently, for she was at heart a kindly old soul as more than one in the household had reason to know.

Whatever the secret might be over which Lollia was giving herself such airs, she could not keep quiet about it. "Something you'd give a pretty to hear, Mary," she would remark apropos of nothing, it seemed to Mary, as they sat with Rufus at his breakfast of barley-meal porridge, "only I'm pledged to silence."

Or she would wag her frowsy old head and pronounce oracularly, "We'll see what we shall see, my lass," or, "It takes time, it takes time." Or as they passed Jupiter's temple on the way to the baker's in the forum to get a quince tart for Rufus to distract him from the pigeons, she would observe piously, "On the knees of the gods, that's where it is, on the knees of the gods."

For the shrines within their own household to Vesta the goddess of the hearth and Janus the god who guarded the door, Lollia was now putting herself to some inconvenience to display a more than dutiful regard, daily offering before them in sacrifice a pinch of sweet-smelling cinnamon borrowed from Ulpian's spice jar or a few drops of perfume from one or another of the lady Livia's various scent vials. "The mistress ought to show more consideration for the gods of her own house," she asserted self-righteously. "All the fragrant balms she has herself rubbed with, she can well spare a little to pleasure Vesta and old Janus."

So nearly on several occasions did Lollia let slip her secret that a question or two from Mary might have loosed the whole story in a flood. But Lollia was given to much talk about affairs of little importance, and Mary had other things upon her mind. For a time Mary had assumed it was to Drusilla's unhappiness at her approaching marriage that Lollia kept making mysterious reference. Lollia was a friend of the family, though considering herself several degrees above Lupinus in social standing. She took no small pleasure in remembering that she used to order him about at will in the days when he was a slave in Sextus' household. Money was not everything, she stoutly maintained, and Lupinus needn't think it was.

Which pronouncement led Mary to believe that Lollia might have some scheme up her sleeve to dissuade Lupinus from wedding Drusilla to the elderly Sejanus. Mary had seen him only once, when Lollia had pointed him out in the forum, one of a group in conversation at the door of a barber shop, a sallow, bald man with a lumpy figure and sharp little eyes.

He was a wealthy man, Lollia said, though you wouldn't think it to see the threadbare toga he wore and old patched shoes. He had made a fortune manufacturing awnings to make shade in the amphitheater from the hot sun. People in even the cheapest seats could rent them; his takings for a single summer afternoon would be more than many an honest, hardworking plebeian was able to earn in the course of a year.

It was not for Sejanus' gold, however, that Lupinus was angling. "As well try to squeeze sap out of last year's broom handle." Lollia despised niggardliness. "Sejanus is miserlier than ever Midas was. It's him that's finagling for the cash, not Lupinus, and no question but he'll get it, Lupinus is so determined to have his daughter titled a lady.

"It's a shabby old bird Lupinus has bagged, but still a knight's a knight, even if he hasn't got a feather left on his poll." Lollia's figures of speech might be mixed, but her meaning was plain.

So that was why Drusilla was having to wed Sejanus. Mary had not realized that he belonged to the equestrian class; there was nothing in his appearance to suggest the nobleman. She felt sorry for Drusilla, but she didn't suppose there was any way for Drusilla to get out of it. If she were in Drusilla's place she wouldn't give in. Rather than have a person like Sejanus for husband she would run away. But Drusilla couldn't—she had not been brought up to hardship, she was timid, she would not know how to earn a living for herself.

Suddenly, as Mary thought about it, it came over her how lucky she was to have learned to stand upon her own feet and fend for herself. It would be agreeable for a while to dwell in a fine villa with servants to wait upon you and ever so many more clothes than you needed and money to spend in the shops for whatever took your fancy. But you'd soon get tired of having nothing to do except try on your newest dress or play a game of knuckle-bones or go for a ride in your litter. Because you couldn't even go walking by yourself if you were rich or if you ranked higher than plebeian; it wasn't proper to go out without a servant or two tagging along. As though you didn't know enough to look after yourself!

Of course things were not all roses if you were poor, but it put you on your mettle and gave you a chance to see what stuff you were made of. You didn't just sit around all day; you were up and doing, and your mind was your own.

"Well, I've done it," Lollia made cryptic confession. "Resorted to a little left-handed magic with Hecate, I mean. Nor don't think it's not on my conscience, Mary"—her complacent smile belied her statement—"because you know quite well I don't sanction black magic. But what with the ides of March almost upon us and Juno and Demeter paying no more attention to my prayers than if I'd never made them a single sacrifice—two offerings of frankincense, and paid for out of my own pocket too— Though with everyone begging favors of them," Lollia interrupted herself to make excuse for the goddesses in case they might be listening, "it's only natural they can't always get around to everybody.

"Anyhow, I'm depending upon Hecate now, and I shouldn't be surprised if before the week is out she manages it that the lord Sextus comes home for a visit." Which, strangely—or perhaps not so strangely, since Sextus had promised to honor Lupinus by attendance at his daughter's wedding—was exactly what came to pass.

Lollia must be conniving to have Sextus take Rufus back with him to Rome, Mary supposed. All winter Lollia had been hoping he would; she would enjoy a change and she wanted to impress Mary with the glories of the great city. Mary couldn't imagine why she had thought it was something to do with Drusilla's wedding that Lollia had had on her mind.

A month ago Mary would have been elated at the prospect of visiting the world's capital, but something like homesickness had been gnawing at her heart and if she were given her choice she would journey to her own country. Not that she would remain there—less than ever now would she be willing to submit her will to Miriam's—but she longed to see her father and baby Saul. Almost a year had passed since last she had seen them, and a year can seem as unending almost as a lifetime.

Sometimes Mary dreamed of the bare little village with the green valley below and the clouds white as lambs pasturing in the blue skies above, and waked to picture to herself how her father's face would shine with gladness to behold her climbing the rocky steep street toward the door. He would run to meet her and embrace her and call her his blue-eyed changeling, the light and life of his house, and other dear words he used to name her by when she was a child. And then she would give him the silver she had saved from her earnings, and he would marvel that it was so large a sum and embrace her again for love and gratitude.

Then Miriam would come running out to see what the excitement was all about, and if the baby Saul held back out of shyness, Mary would coax him with the green-painted crocodile she had bought for him and he would laugh aloud and stretch out his warm little hands to grasp it. And afterwards Simon would summon all the neighbors to celebrate the return of his daughter who had been far across the sea in Italy and now was come safely home, and they would make a feast in her honor. If it was Mark's figure Mary imagined seated beside her at the feast, his voice she heard speaking soft persuasions in her ear, she did not name him to herself, though her heart beat faster.

Nor was the dream Mary had of going home to see her father so improbable as it might seem. The commissions with which Sextus had purposed to send Cordus as emissary to Caesarea and Jerusalem had fallen to Titus. Titus knew better how to deal with publicans and appraise tax records, Sextus decided; Cordus lacked experience.

"Something more important than experience he lacks, Mary, if you want my opinion." Phyllis did not hesitate to say in plain words a thought which Mary was too loyal to Sextus' household to give voice to. "He's an idler, that Cordus, not worth a straw and never will be, and his father may as well face it."

In another fortnight—early in April, when the season of heavy rains was at end and the stormy winds abated that kept the great triremes anchored all winter in port—Titus would set sail. Phyllis would accompany him; she could hardly wait to show her baby son to her family in Sidon— the most wonderful baby, more beautiful than a wall painting, and so intelligent he understood every word you spoke to him.

"He really does, Mary, and it's not just because he's mine that makes me think so. He knows we're talking about him, don't you, my sweet?" Phyllis planted an adoring kiss upon a warm rose-leaf fist.

Only lately, when word had come of Herod's death, had Phyllis considered traveling with her husband to Jerusalem. Not for the whole world would they have risked their infant son within reach of Herod's cruel soldiers. But now Herod was dead, Herod the king who had slaughtered the helpless innocents and slain his own two sons lest they might threaten his throne. No longer was there need to fear for little children since Herod was no more.

Phyllis would like company on the journey; Titus would be busy and you couldn't afford to be too friendly with your slaves. Why couldn't Mary come along? Lollia could surely make out without her for a month or so. And Mary would have an opportunity to visit her family.

As yet Mary had not broached the subject to Lollia, but the more she thought about it the greater her desire to hear her father's voice saying her name, "Mary, my daughter." She was thinking about her father now as she stood before a little bronze mirror in the small room she shared with the old nurse, not quite certain he would approve her spending so much time trying to make herself look elegant. Lollia was already dressed for the wedding but Mary was still busied with her hair, twisting its wavy brown length into intricate glossy coils at the nape of her neck in the latest fashion, as Phyllis had taught her.

"The style of the siren," Phyllis called it. "In honor of Parthenope—you know, the demigoddess of maidens in love.

"And I'll wager a gold fibula against a grain of mustard," she had added, giggling as she showed Mary how to flatten the ringlets against her temple, "that Livia appears with her locks coifed like a siren's too, though she can't be a day younger than fifty." Phyllis often flouted the lady's taste in the matter of dress. Not, of course, when Titus was within hearing. Titus was properly respectful of his master's high-born lady.

It was the first wedding which Mary had ever attended, and when she saw how handsomely some of the guests were attired—upper class friends of Sejanus, no doubt, since it would have been presumptuous of Lupinus to invite them—she felt doubly grateful to Phyllis for instructing her in the art of hairdressing. The ladies held themselves somewhat apart from the others, whether it was custom or because they were superior in rank to the two or three old friends of Paulina, Mary did not know, but she suspected it was because they did not wish to rub elbows with commoners. At the entrance of the lady Livia, however, they had to give ground.

For it pleasured that patrician dame to go sailing past them, scarcely acknowledging their deferential bows and murmured greetings, the folds of her silken gown rustling, her long skirts swishing brilliant buttercup-yellow upon the black and white mosaic of the floor, to salute first the shy, embarrassed Paulina and then Lupinus. Whatever prompted the display of courtesy—whether she wished to put the knights' ladies to shame by affecting a democratic cordiality toward the family of which Sextus was patron, or whether she was really fond of Paulina or perhaps was in an unusually affable mood, having won from Sextus some concession for Cordus' latest debts—Mary was proud to see the lady Livia behave so graciously. The atmosphere in the atrium seemed brighter, people began to look friendlier.

The proper auspices were taken, and Sejanus and Drusilla joined hands before a married friend of Sejanus who acted as priestess. Drusilla was so pretty in her wedding veil of red and dress of fine white crinkled linen with a woolen girdle tied in the "knot of Hercules" that Mary felt sorrier than ever it was not someone younger and pleasanter-looking than Sejanus wearing the bridegroom's wreath of flowers on his head. Stretching as tall as she could to see over Lollia's head, Mary watched the priests make offering to Jupiter of the sacred cake of spelt before they handed it ceremoniously to the bride and groom to partake of. Then there were prayers to the goddess of marriage, the witnesses stepped forward, and the flamen, the priests of Jupiter, signified their approval.

During the wedding feast Mary was several times conscious that Lucius was trying to make her look in his direction, but she would not. If she blushed a little, the candlelight did not betray her. Once when their eyes happened to meet and he smiled, she couldn't help smiling too. But the smile was not for him, she showed him plainly, for she turned her glance quickly away as if it were the wall painting behind him of blackbirds pouncing upon grasshoppers in a clump of green reeds which had caught her attention.

Nor would she stir an inch from Lollia's side during the wedding procession, although Lucius kept motioning her to join the group of young people singing the bridal chant. Why she stuck so close to Lollia she hardly knew. Some part of her pulled at her to make merry with the dancing figures, it was almost impossible to slow her step to Lollia's ambling old-womanish pace, but another part of her held back, pretending not to be interested in the personable figure in the white toga, the cropped blond head so clearly outlined in the glow of the torches.

The evening air was heavy with cold sea mist, the sky hung low, darkness deepened, the torches burned with a sooty, sputtering flame. The three young boys chapleted with laurel who were leading the red-veiled bride to her new home, one going ahead of her, the others at either side, holding her each by a hand, dragged their step, not to bring the happy procession too soon to a close. The groom and his father, the latter so feeble with age he had to be carried in a litter, must be given time to complete the sacrifice they had gone to the temple to make to Jupiter. It would never do for the bride to arrive at the new home before her husband.

Gayer and gayer the flute music flowed through the narrow, darkening street, like silver-toned waters cascading and splashing and spilling over the rim of a fountain, and more and more lively the rhythms of the marriage hymn went round. Even Lollia lifted her voice to add a cracked note to the chorus, and wagged her frizzled head to the beat of the echoing cymbals.

One of the little boys who followed after the bride with her garlanded distaff and spindle stumbled in a groove the chariot wheels had cut in the stone slabs of the pavement, and in the momentary halt while someone helped the child to his feet Mary was aware of a row of figures lined up against a garden wall. The torches flared on their matted hair, their eyes gleamed like coals in hollow eye-sockets, their hands outstretched for alms bony as claws of birds. . . . Beggars . . . half starved and shivering in their rags. Mary shut her eyes to their misery, but she could not shut her mind. She wished she had not seen them. It was not her

fault they were hungry; there was nothing she could do about it.

At the door of his house Sejanus was waiting. The bride touched the doorposts with fat and oil in blessing before he lifted her over the threshold to carry her into the atrium, and the guests came crowding after to ring the hearth where wood was laid for a fire. As Drusilla knelt to kindle the fire with her wedding torch, Lollia and someone else—Mary did not turn her head to see who the second person was, but she was almost sure it was Lucius—pushed Mary to the very front of the ring. She would have been clumsy-fingered indeed not to catch Drusilla's torch when it was extinguished and tossed into the air.

"I s'pose it's too much to expect you to show a little gratitude to the Roman gods," Lollia chided Mary as they undressed that night for bed. "Considering all they've done for you, you ought to be ashamed not to."

Lollia's scolding was sham; she was in high good humor. "It's not every young girl the gods grant a husband so young and handsome, no, not though they bring a dower of gold."

"I don't know what you're talking about," said Mary.

As she spoke the words, however, she felt her face begin to burn, the hot color slide down her neck. Her tone was unconvincing, even to herself. For she did know—or something within her knew. Or at least must have suspected it. Yes, ever since that first day on shipboard when Lucius had shown himself so attentive to her wishes.

"Now don't tell me you didn't know Lucius wants to wed you," Lollia scoffed at the denial. "You'd have to be stone-blind and deaf not to know. Why else do you think he was so insistent I take you to visit his mother and sister in the first place? And that silver fibula you pin your dress with— You didn't for a minute really believe it was I gave it you for Saturnalia gift, did you?

"And if it didn't occur to you Lucius was aiming to have you for wife," Lollia demanded, triumphant as a prosecutor in a court of law presenting incontrovertible evidence, "why do you s'pose he helped me push you out front so you could catch Drusilla's torch?

"Nor you didn't happen to notice"—Lollia's struggle to pull her too tight tunic up over her head made the accusation come in breathy jerks—"that it was at you Drusilla aimed it? There was plenty of others wantin' to grab it first."

"How could I know? About Lucius, I mean." Mary knew herself worsted, she was no match for Lollia in talk. "Nobody said anything to me about it."

"Don't quibble." A born match-maker, Lollia knew no maid lived so modest she could not read the signs by which a young man showed his favor. "But if it hadn't been for me, my girl, your prospects would have snuffed out like a lamp left out in the rain. But we've brought Lupinus 'round to it."

Lollia wanted her share of credit; Mary must not think it was all due to Lucius' stubbornness in refusing to have the wife his father was negotiating to get for him, nor to any persuasion Sextus might have used to convince Lupinus that his son would not be handicapped in his upward climb if he should wed with a commoner.

"It was me turned the trick, Mary, if I say it as I shouldn't —it was me that let Sextus know to take a hand to bring

Lupinus 'round. So Sextus spoke a word to him and promised to stand patron for Lucius.

"Not that Lupinus has aught 'gainst you as a person, Mary, but he'd picked out this run-down knight's daughter to bargain for—ugly as a harpy, Lucius says she is, and cross-grained of temper, though I don't know as I'd take Lucius' word for it—and if it hadn't been for me to smoothen things out, why, I don't doubt Lupinus would have gone through with it and Lucius would have been saddled with her."

Mary was taking the last of the bronze pins from her coiled hair, to braid it for the night. "That was kind of you, Lollia." Her tongue felt clumsy; she could not make her voice sound natural. "I'm grateful to you."

Or was that the word she had meant to use—*grateful?* She could not order her thoughts clearly any more than if she were chasing pell-mell through a rocky field to round up a runaway flock of sheep.

"But I must go home to visit my father. It's already a year, and he'll be disappointed if I don't." It was only her tongue speaking, not herself, making conversation to give her thoughts time to stop churning and whirling and sort themselves out and settle down.

She was embarrassed to have her affairs so public—matters which she had not so much as admitted to her own conscious knowledge—and yet it was undeniably flattering to know herself the object of so much desire. There was a kind of disquiet and uneasiness running through her mind, however, which kept her from enjoying the thought of Lucius and how he had stood out against his father for her sake.

"My baby brother too—I don't want him to forget me." She spoke more loudly than was needful, attempting to drown out the confused voices that seemed to be lifting within her own mind.

"You're sure it's not that fellow Mark that didn't turn a finger to find you while you were in Tyre you're going to see?" Lollia questioned sharply. "You're not intending to stay there?"

"Titus and Phyllis are not sailing to Tyre," Mary made stiff reply. Her face was burning, she shook down her hair to hide it. "And as for my remaining in Judea, my father no longer has need of me. Miriam is mistress of my father's house."

"I'm glad to hear it." Lollia's suspicions were easily allayed. No girl in her right mind would look twice at a poor Judean if it came to a choice betwixt him and a young, handsome Pompeian—and one with a rich father besides. "There's no good comes of postponing marriages when all the auspices are favorable, but likely a few weeks won't make much difference. I'll explain how it is to Lupinus."

Nor was Lollia particularly concerned that the letter which came for Mary with the first ship of the season was from Mark. She watched Mary break the seal, saw her lips set in a straight line, her eyes darken as she scanned the half-score closely written lines.

"After all these months he's got 'round to saying he'll

make arrangements with your father for a betrothal, I s'pose?" Lollia sniffed disdainfully, unashamedly inquisitive. When you get to my age, she would have said, you are entitled to ask questions, especially when they are in the interest of a young person whose future you have undertaken to manage.

"Kept you dangling all this time on a string like a doll in a toy shop and thinks all he has to do when he's a mind to is yank at the knot and down you'll drop right into his hands! Look to it, Mary," she advised, "you don't try to milden things and let him down easy. Tell him point blank you've got better prospects here in Pompeii. He's got it coming to him; he didn't spare your feelings."

"Mark is just someone I've always known, I tell you." As often as Mary had told Lollia, Lollia still insisted otherwise. "It's just a friendly message to let me know he's leaving Tyre to work with a physician in Jerusalem." Which was the truth, though not the whole truth. "He couldn't go there before, on account of Herod." She tore the page in two and dropped the pieces on the floor.

But later, when Lollia took Rufus for a walk in the garden before supper, Mary retrieved the torn fragments and pieced them together to read a second time and a third. Then she folded them carefully into a tiny square to slip within the belt of her dress for safekeeping.

She would not wed Mark, her mind was made up. He need not think he had only to beckon and she would come running. As soon as she had written him a reply she would destroy his letter; she would keep no reminders of him. He could seek him a wife elsewhere to help him work for the cause of the king who was yet too young to know himself a king.

Mark had waited too long; Mary had made other plans and she intended to keep them.

XII

THE THORNBUSH

SINCE THE numbers of Titus' company were few—several clerks and servants, with some six or eight legionaries as guards against highwaymen and thieves—they had joined with a caravan for greater protection. The commissions for the port of Caesarea which Sextus had assigned to Titus had required less than a week to discharge, and already the caravan had traversed more than half the distance overland from the port city to Jerusalem.

Mary was glad when the caravan left the low-lying way of the sea to turn eastward at Lydda toward Jerusalem. The very sight of the hills, solid, immovable, shouldering the azure of the April sky with terraced vineyards and orchards of olive and craggy thickets of wildwood was assurance that this was no dream she was dreaming that she was homeward bound. The hills were real, the clouds of pink and white blossoming almond, the wild iris blue along the rocky watercourses, the sheen of wildflowers among the green grasses of pasture and rough hillslopes.

By actual count it had not been a long journey—ten days on the water from Pompeii to Caesarea, and four days with the caravan. Another two or three days would bring them past Modin and Gibeon to Gibeah, where Mary would part from them while Phyllis continued on with her infant son and Titus to Jerusalem.

But by Mary's count the time had crawled. It was not because she was seasick, like Phyllis—indeed, watching the waves break in endless succession in white crests of foam against the bow of the ship, tasting the salt spray cold on her lips, she could sometimes forget herself and the day's tedium—nor was it because when Phyllis was recovered, they lacked for things to talk about. Nor, curiously, was it Mary's impatience to reach her own village which made the hours creep and drag.

Indeed there were moments when she wondered why she had ever thought she must go home again. It was just a childish notion on her part; she would have done better to remain in Pompeii. Her father was not expecting her so soon; a year from now would have done as well. He had no need of her; he had chosen Miriam to be the light and life of his house. And then Mary would shame herself for so jealous a thought and would go hastily to seek Phyllis' company to keep herself from thinking any thoughts at all.

Sometimes it was of the baby that Phyllis chattered, the latest trick he had surprised her with this morning—wrinkling his little nose and turning his head away because she had forgotten to sweeten the barley gruel she was feeding him. Sometimes she laid plans for his future, how Titus would engage a Greek pedagogue to teach him rhetoric and grammar and logic and the art of oratory and when he was

grown he would make speeches in praise of the emperor
and people would crowd the forum to hear him; or he
would distinguish himself at games and be crowned with
laurel in sight of the crowd; or—if Phyllis happened to be
in a somewhat more practical mood—how he would be so
successful in business and politics that he would be enabled
to enter the ranks of the equites.

"Wouldn't it be wonderful, Mary, if he should wed with
your daughter? For then she'd be a knight's lady, and I'm
sure that would make you proud. Because I don't suppose
by that time Lucius will have been able to get in with the
knights. He's only second generation freedman and Titus
says usually the equestrians won't take them in, no matter
how rich they are, unless they're third generation.

"Though of course with Sextus to back him, Lucius is
bound to be, with Sextus not only a patrician but a friend
of Augustus. And Titus says he thinks Lupinus is down-
right relieved the way things are turning out, though natu-
rally he won't admit it. The bride he had picked for Lucius
was such a scarecrow Lucius might even have divorced her,
and then it would likely have cost Lupinus two or three
times as much to advance Lucius.

"A bride's veil will be wonderfully becoming to you,
Mary. But you must be sure to let me dress your hair so it
shows to best advantage."

Sometimes Mary let Phyllis' talk run pattering past her,
scarcely heard, while she reached over to take the baby into
her own lap to hold him close as if he belonged to her, the

downy black head with its little rumpled red face cradled warm within the hollow of her arm. . . . She would have a house overflowing with children, lively little boys full of mischief, chasing the goats in the pasture and climbing the trees to shake down the figs and racing each other and tussling to see who was strongest and with such appetites you could hardly keep enough bread in the house from one meal to another. One of her little daughters she would call by the name of Damaris, in memory of her own gentle-voiced mother, and to the other she would give the name Martha, because it was a quiet-sounding word which made you think of pleasant, sunny things. The boys she would call by strong, manly names—John and James, Peter and Luke and David.

Nor did it once cross Mary's mind that not one of the names which she would choose was Roman, and that when she imagined herself summoning the children to supper or telling them stories at bedtime about the blackbird that lived in the juniper bush or the little fox cub that ran away, it was always the Aramaic tongue she used, never the Latin.

"Don't you think so, Mary?" Phyllis was questioning. "It's what I've always said about Lucius."

Without knowing what the question had been, Mary agreed, her brown head bent to murmur flattering endearments to the drowsing infant. It might have surprised her, if it had occurred to her, how seldom Lucius came into her thought.

And as likely as not when she did think of him it was in connection with some incident she would as lief not recall— how he had raised his torch in threatening gesture against the beggars lined up beside the wall to watch Drusilla's wedding procession pass, and the angry, desperate eyes the starving creatures had fixed on him as they crowded back out of the way; or how indifferently he shrugged off any suggestion his mother might make, although he was fond of his mother, Mary was certain; and how careful he was not to disturb the pebbles Rufus had laid zigzag across the courtyard but how carelessly that same afternoon he had kicked aside the house of sticks the gardener's little son had been so long in building.

It did no good to remember such things. They were not important; she would put them out of her memory. But in shunting the small incidents out of sight she seemed somehow to have shunted Lucius aside too, almost more completely than she had Mark.

For she had put Mark out of her mind. Or at least she had walled off the part of her mind that had to do with him. He meant nothing to her now; she intended to marry Lucius and live in Pompeii, going home only occasionally to Judea to visit her father and little Saul. . . . It was going to be hard to make her father understand about Lucius—that he wasn't really a pagan, he didn't actually believe in the Roman gods, he only pretended to, like ever so many Romans, because people expected it of him and it was the wish of the emperor that all his people keep up their faith in the old gods.

Though what reply could she make if her father should inquire whether Lucius believed in God? Lucius had laughed a little, the only time the subject had ever been mentioned between them, laughed in that easy-going way he had with people he liked, and had shrugged the question off. Perhaps she should have pressed him to believe, but he had not been interested and it would not have been any use anyhow because she could never find words for the deep things in her mind; she could only feel them. And Lucius was not that kind of person.

Maybe her father would not ask that question. He was not one to speak of deep things any more than she was. It was only Mark, sometimes there in the stony hill pasture as they watched the sheep and listened to the wind's low, sighing music as it passed over thornbush and juniper, could put words to the nameless, half-sad sense of wonder and mystery the sound of the wind stirred in her heart.

"It might be the voice of God that speaks in the wind," Mark had said, so low it might have been her own wistful longing become articulate, "if we could but understand." . . . She must not think of Mark, she would not think of him.

In closing the door of her mind against Mark, however, Mary seemed to have shut herself in. She felt cramped, restless as though she were fettered. There were so many things she must not let herself remember—the sound of Mark's voice, his teasing smile when she was out of temper, the little-boy way the wind ruffled his dark hair, and with what effortless grace he would swing a runaway kid over his shoulder, as debonair of manner as he came striding across the pasture as if he were Jason fetching home the Golden Fleece. . . . Mark could have been what he chose to be—a scholar wise as the elders of the Temple in the knowledge of books, or a physician grown rich in worldly goods from bringing cures to men of power and wealth as Philip of Tyre was urging him to do.

But Mark chose to seek neither honor for himself nor riches. He chose rather to minister to the needy in willing service to the king whose reign in time to come would bring to all men everywhere peace and good will. It might be many years, Mark had written Mary in Pompeii, he might be a gray old man before the new king could take over the rule of the kingdom—that child king who had been cradled in a manger under the star of Bethlehem. In the meantime Mark would endeavor to bring whatever of healing and comfort he was able to those who housed poorer than the fox in his den in the back streets and byways of Jerusalem. For the poor had suffered much under Herod, with none to befriend them.

Mary might have helped Mark with her knowledge of herbs, for Sapphira would have taught her how to prepare healing balms and ointments and which roots and barks to steep for medicines. But Mark had delayed too long to have any right to expect it of her now. While he had been mak-

ing his plans, she had made hers. There was no reason for
her to change now just because he had said in his letter that
he had sent word to his father to arrange for their betrothal.
He need not think she would remain always at his beck and
call. Besides, what had Mark to offer her more desirable
than to be mistress of a fine villa with plenty of servants
to do her bidding and some day the privilege of being titled
a lady?

She would not think of Mark; she would put him out of
her mind. She would never see him again. Except once—
just once more—when he had grown old and gray and
bowed with years they would meet by chance on a street
in Jerusalem. She would not have recognized him, he was
so changed, but even in her fine Roman clothes he would
know her from afar because the years had dealt so lightly
with her. And picturing to herself the sadness in Mark's eyes
as he told how all this long, long time he had remained true
to her, and thinking to herself how for her sake he had
dwelt alone and lonely with none to care for him, Mary
had to hide her face a moment against the baby's swaddled
feet lest Phyllis might see the tears she could not blink back.

"He's sound asleep," she whispered, swallowing a kind
of knot in her throat, "the baby, I mean. I'll go for a walk,
to stretch my feet after so long in the saddle."

"Only a short distance," Phyllis cautioned, matronly as if
she were Mary's mother. "It'll soon be dusk, there might be
robbers. And I smell supper beginning to cook."

The caravan had struck camp near a spring that bubbled

from beneath a grass-grown ledge below the trail. It was a shallow pool, drying up with the grasses soon after the rainy season came to an end, but while it lasted the water was fresh and good. Mary would have liked to have a drink and wash her hands and face clean of dust but the cook's dark-skinned scullions were crowding to fill bronze vessels and leather buckets, and several camel men, their turbans and thin cotton jackets colored with sandy dust, were waiting their turn to quench their thirst. Perhaps if she walked a little way up the gulley in the opposite direction she might find another place to drink.

A thin trickle of water gave soggy footing to a bed of green rushes, sedges bent and swayed in the light breeze, and a warbler perched on a sprig of thorn to whistle his mate from her nest in a tree of wild olive, his call soft as the notes the shepherds play on their reed pipes when they lead the flocks down from the hills at folding time.

The sun was low, drawing out the shadows of reeds and rushes, the long shafts of level light lifting the feathery grasses out of anonymity for a fleeting hour to stand individual in airy form and grace. Mary's steps led through a patch of wild thyme, and the pungent sweet scent as it crushed under her sandals wakened memories sharp as blades in her heart.

She might have gone no further up the narrow wadi—lush green now in April but dry and bare in summer as the stones with which it was strewn—had she not glimpsed, a few yards beyond, something she had never before beheld—

a bush with thorns all shining gold. It was a thornbush,
there was no mistaking the scraggy stiff growth, and there
were buds on the spines of the thorn, buds that put her in
mind of the jewels the lord Sextus had fetched the lady
Livia from some far eastern land, lustrous as drops of green
sea-water.

Of course it could not be true gold, the bush, because no
such thing ever grew, but it was so beautiful she could not
be satisfied with looking. She must touch it, assure herself
it was not something she imagined. Even though it was no
more than the reflected gold of sunset she would never
have believed so coarse and common a thing as a thornbush
could become a thing of beauty.

The wadi widened to a shallow glade, carpeted with grass
and pale convolvulus. A donkey grazed on the herbage, and
a man in an old brown cloak such as shepherds wear was
dipping a leather bowl in a pool fringed with blue lilies.
Beneath a gnarled tree a woman was resting, a piece of
ragged carpet spread to cushion the ground where she sat,
the hems of her blue mantle gilded with the low sunlight.
A child slept in her arms, his hair soft gold against her
shoulder.

As Mary gazed, unnoticed there by the thornbush, she
felt a gradual quietness well up within her mind. Her rest-
lessness fell away, her sense of frustration, the unsatisfied
yearning for she knew not what. These were people like
herself, their poverty was dear to her. Like her, they too

were returning from some far journey, after long absence
among strangers.

How it was, Mary could not have told, nor why it should
be, but to come thus in that peaceful solitude upon the

weary young mother and sleeping child, the father their living shield and shelter, and to know the little family kin to her in hope and need and longing, was to feel a weight being lifted from her heart, chains struck off which had bound her, gates and doors flung wide which had been locked and barred.

There in that clear golden April light Mark's words came back to her, words spoken on an afternoon serene with sunset as this, words whose meaning had been dark to her because her mind was closed against them. Life is not given to us to be lived for ourselves alone, he had said in his quiet way. What we can do to help others, that we must. Not because of any commandment or compulsion which has been laid upon us, but willingly, out of love.

She had been blind, and now she could see. She had been divided against herself—she could see it now—she had all but surrendered her very self. She had been lost, and now she was found.

"The water is cool and sweet, Mary. Shall I fetch you a cup to drink?"

Had the man's back not been turned, Mary might have thought it was to her he was speaking. It was to his wife he was offering the cup, there where she sat under the wild olive with the child cradled in her arm, the low branches arching in leafy canopy above her head.

"We drank not in Egypt of springs so refreshing, Joseph," her soft voice thanked him as she tasted the cup.

It was from Egypt, then, that the little family was returning, having gone there to dwell perhaps out of fear of Herod, but now, like Phyllis and Titus, no longer afraid for their child, since Herod was dead. Of what lineage they might be or to what village they were coming home, Mary did not know, and yet—although she knew she must be mistaken—the mild, sweet face of the young mother seemed not unknown to her. Once before, upon some distant time and occasion, it must be that she had beheld the mother and child. . . . But she would have remembered if she had. Nor could she ever have seen them before, since she had not been in the land of Egypt. Perhaps it was because they were of her own country and her own people that they seemed not strange to her.

As Mary gazed, forgetful of herself and the rough ground where she stood, the other Mary lifted her eyes and saw her standing by the thornbush and smiled a gentle smile to see her regard them so earnestly.

Their eyes met, and for a moment it was as though time reached out to touch eternity, so swift and illimitable was the joy which Mary felt surge up within her. Some part of her, deeper than thought or senses, deep as her very being, felt the golden light flood through her, heard the winds call her with the voices of friends. She was one with the silver song of the warbler skimming the reed bed, one with the bending and swaying rushes. The very stones were her brothers, and she was sister to mountains and stars and to all living things. It was God's hand which had made them all and would hold them ever safe in his keeping.

The vision faded, but something remained—a healing sense of being at one with herself and of how good it is to be alive, with work to do in the world—brave, homely work which life had set for Mark and her together.

The father, Mary saw, was taking from the saddlebag a wrapped loaf to break for their supper. Quietly, not to disturb the sleeping child, Mary made her way down the ledge. Once she stopped to look back, and then walked on. The shadows were lengthening, the bullfrogs were beginning their evening chant, a flight of swallows twittered overhead.

In another few months, Mark had written—a six-month at the most—the Tyrian Philip would have taught him all he could of the art of surgery and medicine. And then Mark would make his way speedily to Jerusalem, from whence he would come to fetch Mary to be his wife, so soon as ever she returned from Pompeii. . . . And the doors of our house, Mary thought to herself as she followed the dwindling green line of reeds and sedges down the wadi in that late sunlit hour, the doors of our house will never be closed against those who sorrow.

There would be times when things went wrong and she would lose her temper and perhaps hurt the feelings of her little daughters, and scold the little boys because they had torn their tunics or lost the penny she had given them to buy oil for the lamp. There would be times when she would

be wishful for the soft, easy life of Pompeii, for garments of
fine cloth and silver to spend as she pleased and servants to
do her bidding. But she would have something better than
gold could buy, something she would not exchange for all
the world's riches.

And all that she remembered would still be her own—the
lord Sextus' stately villa with its fountains and its gardens
that looked off toward the sparkling blue sea, the colon-
naded forum where the togaed Pompeians strolled and
chatted, and little Rufus chasing the pigeons on the porch
of Jupiter's temple, as valiant and cheerful as though his
lame foot were sound. Yes, and old Lollia, brusque of tongue
and kindly of heart; Drusilla, with her fair hair caught up
in a silver net, and the pleasant-voiced Paulina.

And Lucius too, who had befriended her and singled her
out to show her especial favor, friendly, handsome Lucius
whose ambition it was to become a rich nobleman privileged to wear a gold ring upon his finger—Lucius would
find himself a bride more suitable to him than Mary. For
his way lay remote from her way, and his thoughts could
never be her thoughts.

As Mary approached the camp she smelled fresh bread
baking upon hot stones, a haunch of venison roasting with
a delicious savory odor upon the spit. She was hungry; a
piece of bread and a few dried figs had been her sole refreshment at midday.

It was good to see the fires glimmering beneath the blackened cauldrons, the tired pack-animals grazing their fill on

the tall grass, and men sitting cross-legged to rest beside the spring as in her own village at the going down of the sun, when they had brought the flocks down from the hill pastures to the folding, the shepherds sat them to rest under the old sycamore beside the spring.